W9-CAU-599

"Are you a fighter?" Chancy suggested. "Or just a Saturday night drunk?"

The prisoner came off the bunk fast. "Open that damned door," he said, his jaw set.

"You?" Chancy sneered. "Why I'd pin back your ears, grease your hair and swallow you whole. If you ever take a punch at me I'll bounce you so high they'd have to shoot you to keep you from starving to death."

The prisoner chuckled suddenly. "Open the door, boss. You've hired yourself a boy."

OTIS CHANCY WAS ONLY NINETEEN, BUT HE WAS TRAIL BOSS OF THE HARDEST OUTFIT IN THE WEST—AND ALREADY HE HAD BOUGHT A PACK OF MAN-SIZED TROUBLE!

CHANCY

LOUIS L'AMOUR

BENDIGO SHAFTER
BORDEN CHANTRY
BRIONNE
THE BROKEN GUN
THE BURNING HILLS
THE CALIFORNIOS
CALLAGHEN
CATLOW
CHANCY
THE CHEROKEE TRAIL
COMSTOCK LODE
CONAGHER
CROSSFIRE TRAIL
DARK CANYON
DOWN THE LONG HILLS
THE EMPTY LAND
FAIR BLOWS THE WIND
FALLON
THE FERGUSON RIFLE
THE FIRST FAST DRAW
FLINT
GUNS OF THE TIMBERLANDS
HANGING WOMAN CREEK
THE HAUNTED MESA
HELLER WITH A GUN
THE HIGH GRADERS
HIGH LONESOME
HONDO
HOW THE WEST WAS WON
THE IRON MARSHAL
THE KEY-LOCK MAN
KID RODELO
KILKENNY
KILLOE
KILRONE
KIOWA TRAIL
LAST OF THE BREED
LAST STAND AT PAPAGO WELLS
THE LONESOME GODS
THE MAN CALLED NOON
THE MAN FROM SKIBBEREEN
THE MAN FROM THE BROKEN HILLS
MATAGORDA
MILO TALON
THE MOUNTAIN VALLEY WAR
NORTH TO THE RAILS
OVER ON THE DRY SIDE
PASSIN' THROUGH
THE PROVING TRAIL
THE QUICK AND THE DEAD
RADIGAN
REILLY'S LUCK
THE RIDER OF LOST CREEK
RIVERS WEST
THE SHADOW RIDERS

SHALAKO
SHOWDOWN AT YELLOW BUTTE
SILVER CANYON
SITKA
SON OF A WANTED MAN
TAGGART
THE TALL STRANGER
TO TAME A LAND
TUCKER
UNDER THE SWEETWATER RIM
UTAH BLAINE
THE WALKING DRUM
WESTWARD THE TIDE
WHERE THE LONG GRASS BLOWS

SHORT STORY COLLECTIONS
BOWDRIE
BOWDRIE'S LAW
BUCKSKIN RUN
DUTCHMAN'S FLAT
THE HILLS OF HOMICIDE
LAW OF THE DESERT BORN
NIGHT OVER THE SOLOMONS
THE RIDER OF THE RUBY HILLS
RIDING FOR THE BRAND
THE STRONG SHALL LIVE
THE TRAIL TO CRAZY MAN
WAR PARTY
WEST FROM SINGAPORE
YONDERING

SACKETT TITLES BY LOUIS L'AMOUR
SACKETT'S LAND
TO THE FAR BLUE MOUNTAINS
THE WARRIOR'S PATH
JUBAL SACKETT
RIDE THE RIVER
THE DAYBREAKERS
SACKETT
LANDO
MOJAVE CROSSING
MUSTANG MAN
THE LONELY MEN
GALLOWAY
TREASURE MOUNTAIN
LONELY ON THE MOUNTAIN
RIDE THE DARK TRAIL
THE SACKETT BRAND
THE SKY-LINERS

NONFICTION
FRONTIER
A TRAIL OF MEMORIES:
    The Quotations of Louis L'Amour,
    compiled by Angelique L'Amour

CHANCY
LOUIS L'AMOUR

BANTAM BOOKS
TORONTO • NEW YORK • LONDON • SYDNEY • AUCKLAND

CHANCY

A Bantam Book / April 1968
2nd printing ...... *May 1969* 4th printing ... *October 1969*
3rd printing ...... *June 1969* 5th printing ... *February 1970*
6th printing ... *August 1970*
New Bantam edition / October 1971
2nd printing ... *August 1973* 12th printing ..... *June 1979*
3rd printing ..... *May 1974* 13th printing ..... *April 1980*
4th printing ..... *May 1975* 14th printing ... *August 1980*
5th printing ... *August 1975* 15th printing ... *October 1981*
6th printing . *December 1975* 16th printing ... *August 1982*
7th printing ..... *June 1976* 17th printing ... *August 1983*
8th printing ..... *May 1977* 18th printing ..... *July 1984*
9th printing . *November 1977* 19th printing ... *August 1985*
10th printing .. *February 1978* 20th printing ..... *April 1986*
11th printing ..... *June 1978* 21st printing .. *February 1987*
22nd printing ... *January 1988*

*Photo of Louis L'Amour by
John Hamilton—Globe Photos, Inc.*

ISBN 0-553-25580-0

Published simultaneously in the United States and Canada

*Bantam Books are published by Bantam Books, a division of
Bantam Doubleday Dell Publishing Group, Inc. Its trademark,
consisting of the words "Bantam Books" and the portrayal of
a rooster, is Registered in U.S. Patent and Trademark Office
and in other countries. Marca Registrada. Bantam Books,
666 Fifth Avenue, New York, New York 10103.*

PRINTED IN THE UNITED STATES OF AMERICA

KR   31 30 29 28 27 26 25 24 23

To the men of
THE UNITED STATES ARMED FORCES . . .
wherever they may be

CHANCY

When I rode out of the timber I fell in with a cow out-fit, and a sorry lot of rawhiders they were.

They had a fire going and coffee on, and the smell of the coffee and of bacon frying fairly set my stomach to asking questions of my face. I'd come a far piece with nothing to chew on but my thoughts.

When I came up to the fire not one of them upped to say aye, yes, or no. They just sat there looking beat. This was a played-out hand if ever I saw one.

"Howdy," I said. "You folks taking on any help?"

There was a thin, stooped-down man, with every bone showing through his thin cotton shirt, who looked around at me. If that man's cattle were as poor as he was, there'd not be fat enough on ary one of them to grease a skillet.

"Was I to hire you, I couldn't pay. We're fresh out of everything a man needs most."

Well, I could have fetched him some ideas on that score, because I'd already seen the girl who stood with her back against the chuck wagon.

"Where you driving the herd?"

"We ain't. Not no more. We were headed for a valley out yonder where the grass stands high. Now it looks like we ain't a-goin' anywhere at all."

"What happened?"

"Sheriff in this town lays claim to a bunch of our cattle. Swears they're local brands."

"Ain't the cattle yours?"

"Rightly they are, but there's a point of question and the sheriff knows it. Cattle have been running on Texas grass since Spanish days, with nobody laying claim to hide nor hair of them. Folks branded a few of them, but the War between the States cut that short, so they just ran free and bred free. We made a gather of them, and started north.

"We had a few brands among them. Men died during the war, and then in the Injun fightin' an' such. These brands we have nobody laid claim to, and we honestly tried to run them all down. Now this man claims they're local cattle that drifted south."

"All the way to Texas?" I said. "Swimming those rivers and all? It ain't likely. Away out west it might happen, but there's too much good grass around here for cows to leave it. He's running a bluff on you."

"You et, son? I got no kind of job for you, but no man ever walked away from Noah Gates's fire without he'd et if he was a mind to."

All I owned was on my back or on my horse. That excepts a lay of ridge-country land back in Tennessee, and the offer of that meal sounded fresh and likely to me. So I out with my skinning knife and edged up to the fire, helping myself to beef and beans.

Nobody had much to say as they moved to the fire to partake. It looked to me as if this outfit was fresh out of hope and gumption, as well as other things. They were oldish men, most of them with families at home, likely, and wondering what their womenfolks would do if they didn't come back.

They weren't the frontier type of man. These were the second string, and good men often enough, but hard work and bad crops or bad luck had probably wiped out their efforts, and had taken away a good deal of their will to fight back.

Only a few weeks before I'd left the faraway hills of Tennessee to make myself a place in the world, and when I finally taken off there was nothing left in the cabin but a chunk of side meat off a razor-back hog and some fresh ground meal. I taken that grub and rattled my hocks out of there.

When I rode up to this cow outfit I was three days without eating except for some hazelnuts I'd found, but the longer I sat there listening to their talk the more it seemed to me that this sheriff, as he called himself, was running a blazer on Gates and his outfit. The worst of it was, he looked likely to make it stick. Now, I was just a riding-through stranger, but I'd set up to good grub for the first time in days, and I didn't like to think of some no-account running me away from the trough.

Back in my mountains, folks run long on fighting. A man may not have much, but he sets store by his pride as a free-born American citizen, and is ready to fight for what he believes, you choose the time and place.

Back in the hills when you'd hunted 'coon, drunk a little 'shine, and courted the girls, there wasn't much else to do but fight. Now, I never cared much for the jug, but I was a fair hand at courting. But with me it was mostly the fighting. It was just fighting in good spirits, knuckle and skull, root-hog-or-die kind of fighting among us boys. And what these folks needed right now was the will to fight.

Only that honed no blades for me. Pa, he always said a man had to look spry for himself, because nobody would do it for him; your opportunities didn't come knocking around, you had to hunt them down and hogtie them. Maybe it was that idea I was considering, and maybe it was the beans in the pot, or it might have been that redhead girl standing over there casting eyes at me, time to time.

So I spoke free, and I told them were they my cows nobody would take them without they had a fight.

"Ain't much we can do," Gates said. "That sheriff's a mighty hard man, and it's a hard lot he has with him. Even if we got shut of this place, there's nothing but Injuns west, and trouble of every kind."

"What about that valley with the tall grass?" I asked.

"Maybe that was just a dream. Anyway, none of us ever saw it. A passing stranger told us of it—a roving man by the name of Sackett, far riding from the western lands."

"If a Sackett told you that valley was there, it was there," I said, me being kin of theirs, although distant.

Now, I was doing some contemplating. This here wasn't an organized state yet, so there weren't any county officials, and no sheriffs. Getting the herd together had taken the last bit of gumption these men had, and the long, hard trail drive had worn them down and whipped them. And I was betting that town outfit had seen that very thing.

"Mr. Gates, what brands were they about to take?"

"Circle Three, Ten Bar, Shamrock, and Slash Seven. That adds up to about half the herd."

Well, a man doesn't look on opportunity too often, and even though the deck was stacked against them, I felt like taking a hand. "Mr. Gates," I said, "you sell those brands to me. You sell them to me right now."

"Sell them? Son, you got that kind of money?"

"No, sir. I haven't got a cent, but I'll give you a handwrit note for one thousand dollars for those cows, all the brands you've named, sight unseen."

"You're talkin' foolish, boy."

"You want my note for a thousand dollars, or you want nothing? That's what they'll leave you. Looks to me as if you've got to fight or quit. Now I'm giving you something else. You sell those cows to me and the fight becomes mine."

"They'll ride rough-shod over you, boy."

"Sell to him." The speaker was a burly, sort of fat

man with a stubble of beard over a weak chin. "What can we lose?"

Then we heard the sound of their horses, and it seemed to me Gates turned a shade sicker than he had been before. "I'll write a bill of sale," I said. "All you've got to do is sign it."

There were six men with that so-called sheriff. To me he was just a thief wearing a stolen badge, and those with him were a mean, shifty-looking lot, but hard men, every one of them.

"We've come to make our cut by daylight, Gates. You just stand aside and there'll be no trouble."

"The cattle belong to us," Gates said. "We gathered them down on the Trinity."

The sheriff just grinned, a taunting, ugly kind of a grin. Oh, he'd sized them up, all right! He knew this outfit had no heart for a fight.

So I taken a letter from my pocket, and on the back of a page of that letter I wrote: *In consideration of $1,000 payable when the herd is sold, I hereby sell and release title to all Circle Three, Ten Bar, Shamrock, and Slash Seven cattle to the bearer of this note.*

When I handed Gates that note, he looked from them to me. He was scared, but he dearly hated to sell.

"It's better than nothing," I said, "and that's what he'll leave you." I handed him the pencil. "Just sign it."

"What's going on here?" the sheriff demanded. "What's that paper?"

"All right, all right," Gates whispered hoarsely to me. "They're yours." He glanced at the others with him. "You agree?"

They nodded, and he signed.

Deliberately I took the paper, turned my back on them, and walked to my horse. Tied to the saddle by a slipknot was my Colt revolving shotgun. Taking the shotgun, I stepped back into the light.

"What's goin' on here?" the sheriff said again. "What d'you think you're doin'?"

"I just bought title to those cattle you say you're going to cut from the herd. You ain't getting hide nor hair of them. Now, you boys just turn yourselves around and ride back to town."

He looked to be a mighty mean man, and I knew he wasn't going to back down. At the beginning, before he started to run his bluff, they might have kept him off; but once he'd gotten a toe hold it meant a fight.

"Now, see here, boy!" He started to turn his horse to bring his rifle to bear, and I let him turn until the muzzle started to lift, then I shot him out of the saddle.

That Colt shotgun was loaded with buckshot, and it cut loose with a tremendous roar. That so-called sheriff left his saddle as if he'd been pole-axed.

The rest of them sat almighty still, afraid to blink for fear I'd shoot again. There was no arguing with that shotgun, and I held the drop. My next step took me nearer, but also deeper into the shadows near a wagon.

"Pick him up," I said, "and ride out of here. I'll kill the next man on sight that I see."

Well, sir, they done it. They got down mighty meek and hung him over the saddle and then they rode out of there, and they seemed pleased to be going.

On the ground where the body lay was a six-shooter that had fallen from his belt. I went over and picked it up. It was a finely made gun with an oddly carved ivory butt. Holding it up, I called after them, but they were gone, and they were not about to come back, so I thrust that gun back of my belt, and with that move I bought a ticket to hell with a dead man's gun.

Gates's men just sat there, too surprised and shocked to speak. "They've gone," Gates said finally; "you ran them off."

Me, I walked to the fire and picked up my cup. I was shaking a mite, and I didn't want them to see it. Boy though I was, I'd had a spell of time to know something of men, and knew my troubles had only begun.

"You killed him," one of the men said, as if he couldn't believe it.

"He came yearning for it."

"But you killed him!"

I drank my coffee. Sitting there by the fire, I could see the idea was beginning to reach them. The danger was over—it was gone. But now there was something else. I owned half their herd.

And I had killed a man, something I'd never done before, and hoped not to do again. It left me feeling sickish in the stomach, but I knew I daren't let them know it.

There by the wagon wheel, that redhead girl was looking at me. She wasn't smiling, and she wasn't offering any friendliness. She was just looking.

"Seems to me," I said, "We'd better move this herd. We'd best put some distance behind us."

They stared at me. The youngest of the men could have been my grandpa.

"Did you have to shoot that man?" one of them said. "Did you have to kill him?"

"What would you have done?"

Nobody answered that question, so I finished my coffee and, taking up my fixings, walked back to my horse.

We had to get moving, but the men had already started to think. They hadn't come to any decision yet, but they would. Just give them time.

2

We moved the cattle west a good eight miles, then bedded down, and all night long a soft rain fell. In the morning I rode out to make tally of my cattle.

The night guard came to me. He was Harvey Bowers, a lean, bitter old man with a skimpy face and thin hair stretched hard over his skull. "What you huntin' for?" he asked.

"Studyin' my cattle. Makin' a tally, if you want to know."

"Ain't yours yet. Not until you pay that note." He rolled his quid in his lean jaws. "You got a long way to go, boy."

"I've been there before. I been over the trail."

"You come by them cattle mighty easy. It taken us months of hard work to make the gather."

"And you could have lost them in one minute. If you figured it was easy to keep them, you could have tried. I risked my hide for them, don't forget that."

The cattle were in fair shape, better than I had expected. They had come up the Shawnee Trail, the roughest of the lot, with deep rivers to swim, and lots of broken country and brush, but the grass had been good, and with the rains and all, they'd had a-plenty to drink.

But now trouble was shaping up for me. A big share of the herd was mine if I made good on that note, and the thought of it was beginning to rankle with those men. Boy I might be, but I was wise enough to know that, given time, every man jack of them would come to hate me.

The rain was a mesh of steel against an iron sky. We pointed the herd west down a valley of grass where a small stream wound among the willows and redbud. This was Indian country, but the Indians were friendly . . . it was said. The Cherokees were friendly, I knew, and good people, but they had their renegades, too, and a herd of strange cattle would be a temptation to them.

Westward, the Indians we would meet would be wild Indians, out for scalps and horses, and I had an idea this rawhide outfit would be glad they had me along. But I knew that folks can sometimes come to hate a man they owe; and as time went on, they would find reasons for liking me less and less.

When I came in to the fire at noontime they had been talking about it. There was no friendship for each other among these men, only a kind of cold toleration.

Taking hold of the pot, I used my left hand. Gates looked up at me from his seat on the ground. "Young, ain't you?"

"Nineteen," I said, "nineteen by two months, but don't let the years fool you. I've covered country."

"You killed that man mighty easy. You killed men before?"

"I've been shot at, and shot back. I never took to counting scalps."

"That was a lawman you killed."

"He lied when he told you that. This is Indian Territory, and the law is the United States Marshal and his deputies."

The coffee was good, I'll say that for them. "You

got off easy," I said. "Once that outfit got away with
the cattle they claimed, they'd have come back for the
rest." I glanced over their heads at that redhead girl.
"And that wouldn't have been all they'd have taken."

After that they talked among themselves, leaving me
out, so when I'd finished eating I saddled up and returned to the drive.

Now, I'd never asked anything of anybody, nor expected anything from folks. Nobody could be held to
account for what his people did or didn't do, but I'd
had to answer for pa.

Pa was hung for a horse thief when I was a tall
thirteen. After a lifetime of hard work and self-denial,
in which pa had few of the things he set store by, he
had made one foolish mistake and got hung for it.

It was never in me to judge a man, because each of us
does his share of sinning, one way or another. Other
folks prospered and pa didn't, but it was no fault of his
that I could see, although that cut no ice with the folks
down on the flatlands. They called him shiftless and no-
account because he was poor, but pa had never been
either of those things. But they hung him by the neck
and made me stand to watch. To teach me a lesson,
they said.

"You stand and watch, boy. This is what comes to
thieves."

You'd think there'd have been some Christian kind-
ness in them, but there wasn't an ounce. It was Martin
Brimstead whose horse was stolen, and there was no
sympathy in the man, nor any understanding, and some
say he even wore a name he'd no right to. He was there
to see the job was done, but the man who led the mob
was Stud Pelly. And it was Stud Pelly who grabbed me
and twisted my head, forcing me to look at pa, hanging
there.

When it was all over they just walked off and left me
standing there, and I climbed the tree to cut pa
down . . . he was dead, all right, a good kind man

gone . . . and then old man Dunvegan came up the
road, and he took pa's body as I lowered it down, holding him in his arms to ease him to the ground.

"It was the drink did it, boy," he said. "Your pa was
no drinking man, and had no head for it. He'd been
standing off sighing for that horse for a year or two, so
when he got a couple of drinks in him he just mounted
up and rode around.

"It was a mistake he made, and with the wrong man.
There's no forgiveness in Martin Brimstead . . . and that
Stud Pelly, he'd hang any man he could hang legal.
He's got the taste of blood in his mouth."

Dunvegan helped me to bury pa, and arranged for me
to travel down the country with a pack peddler. After
that I lived hand to mouth around Charleston for six
months or so, holding various jobs and learning what
the outside world was like. Then I went up to Boston
as a ship's boy, down to New Orleans as a sailor before
the mast, and up the river to Natchez and St. Louis on
river boats.

After a while—four years it was—I hankered for the
mountains and followed the Trace back over the rough
country into the Smokies. The cabin pa and me had
called home was still there in the clearing near the tall
pine, and the grass stood high all about as if nobody
had been near the place since.

By the time I'd cleaned out the cabin and the well, I
was getting low on supplies that I'd packed in over the
back trail along Chancy Ridge—named for pa—so I
walked the old Cherokee trails to the flat lands to buy
seed corn and supplies. I also bought me a brown mule
to pack it.

Most of the Cherokees had been forced to leave their
lands and move west to Indian Territory, and their trails
were no longer used except by some hunter or an Indian
from afar. Not many of the flatlanders knew of those
trails up there along the ridges, so I could come and go
with nobody bothering their heads about me.

After I spaded the garden plot, I plowed up a patch for seed corn, and did my planting.

Sometimes of a nighttime I'd get to yearning after folks and I'd walk away out on Chancy Point to look down into the valley where I could see the lights of homes. Nobody down there wanted to see me—they'd think of me as that horse thief's boy, if at all.

Of course—and the thought kept a-nagging—there was old Jerry Dunvegan. He'd been friendly when no one else would be, when I was a scared, heart-broke boy.

It was lonesomeness started me down the mountain, and an evil day it was when I decided to call on old Jerry.

The mule taken me down. The night was a quiet one, with a sliver of moon holding its shadow in its arms, and the darkling pines were a fringe along the sky. A ghost wind moved among the trees when I rode down to the village that had hung my pa, down to see the one man I could call friend.

His house stood nigh the brook that tumbled down the mountain from my own ridge, and a white cow looked over the rail fence at us as we came by, with the barn and the barn smells close to hand. It was when I was turning in at the gate, with what surmising I could only guess at, that I turned and rode back and tethered my mule in the pines near the brook.

Closing the barnyard gate behind me, I went to the kitchen door and tapped light. There was a moment of stillness within, then a footstep and a voice. "Who's there?"

"A friend, inquiring for Jerry Dunvegan."

The door opened a bit, and a woman stood inside. It was Jerry's oldest, a tall, thin girl, looking out at me. "I don't know you. Who is it, calling on pa?"

"It's Otis Tom . . . Otis Tom Chancy, ma'am."

She kind of caught her breath, and her features stiffened as she looked at me. "Go away from here!" she said. "You've caused trouble enough!"

"I'm sorry, ma'am, but Mr. Dunvegan treated me kindly. I thought to bring him thanks, and news of me."

"Go away! He's had his fill of you, and so have we all. Befriended you, did he? And a sight of trouble it caused. When they found out—"

Her voice was getting high, and sound carried in the still night air, which made me nervous. "If you'd let me step in—" I began.

She drew back. "Never let up on him, they didn't. They read him out of the church, and nobody'd take to him at all. That was Brimstead's doing."

"I'd no idea. Your pa was Christian kind to me, ma'am, when I was a boy alone, and—"

"You get out now. I've told you what trouble you caused, and if they knew you'd come here again they'd be meaner than ever."

"Can I see Jerry?"

"No, you can't see him. Pa's abed."

The door behind her opened a mite, and a slim bit of a girl was standing there. It was Kitty Dunvegan, old Jerry's youngest, scarcely fourteen.

"Kit, you get back!" the tall girl said. "And close that door!"

"Who is it, Priss?"

"It's that no-account Otis Tom, the horse thief's boy." She turned on me, fiercely angry. "Now you get, or I'll call Stud Pelly."

It was no use. Stepping back from the door, I said, "Sorry ma'am, I just wanted to see your pa. He stood by me. And you know, ma'am, *I* never stole any horses. I don't deny pa was up on that horse. He was drunk at the time, and him unaccustomed to strong drink. When he sobered up he'd have taken that horse back, with apologies. He was that kind of man. Trouble was, Brimstead and Stud, they wanted a hanging, and they got it."

"That makes no difference. Your pa stole that horse, and Mr. Brimstead's an important man. Why, he owns nigh half the county!"

When the door closed I held still a minute, listening.

Then I went through the barnyard, climbed over the fence, and made it to my mule.

Behind me a door closed, so I sat my saddle, listening. Who could that be, I wondered. It had sounded like the Dunvegan door.

Time was a-wasting, so I walked my mule off up through the trees, only returning to the trail after I'd put half a mile behind me. It was fetching up to daybreak when I reached the cabin.

A mite hungry, I put a fire together and started to fry some hog-meat, when of a sudden I heard a whisper of sound from outside. Having no cause to expect friendship in a place where so many held hatred for me, I caught up my gun and stepped to the door.

A girl was coming across the yard from the woods. Not from the path, but from the brook. Now a body could come up from the village that way, and much faster than by the path, but it was a climb and a scramble among rocks and brush. It was that skinny Dunvegan girl . . . the young one.

"Kit," I said, "what are you doing up here?"

"Priss told them. I came to warn you. She told Stud and them, and they're fixing to come for you . . . the lot of them."

"Why? I never did anything wrong."

"That don't make no difference to them. Stud's talking it up that they want no thief's kin around here. He's got his rope, but he says you'll get a whoppin' and a running start. He's all the time talking about that rope. It hung one man, he says, and if need be it'll hang others. Folks are afraid of him."

"You borrowed trouble, Kit. You shouldn't have come. Now, what did you do that for?"

She dug her toe in the ground. "Pa likes you. Priss didn't speak true, because I know pa would have wished to see you. It's true folks have treated us shabby, but pa's proud, and he pays them no mind. It's cost us a-plenty, because nobody would do business with pa.

Some didn't like what he did, but most of them were just afraid to cross Brimstead."

"You get back before they find out," I told her.

"What will you do?"

"I could run, but I'm of no mind for it. I'll wait and let them speak their piece. If worse comes to worst, I can get out."

She was a slim youngster, and she had come far to warn me, so I taken her by the chin and kissed her lightly on the cheek. "You go along now," I said, "but you tell your pa I'll never forget what he did, and if he ever needs a friend, he's only to sing out and I'll come runnin'."

She was gone in a moment, slipping into the woods like a wraith. And they were coming.

From the sound of them I knew where they were on the trail, and as there seemed to be time enough, I led my mule around and down by my sneaky trail and hid him in the brush below the cabin where the rock wall fell sheer away from the cabin foundation. I tied him there and went back and filled my water bucket.

When I heard their voices to, I stepped back inside and barred the door, then closed the shutters and barred them, opening only the loop holes. From the back window, which they could neither approach nor see, I hung a rope where I could slide down to the mule.

There looked to be nine or ten of them, mostly loafers and no-accounts.

"You!" came a voice. "In the house there!" That was Stud Pelly. He was a big man, not taller than most, but wider and thicker, a strong, mean man with the name of being a bully. "Come on out of there!"

I just sat there, a-watching and a-waiting. It was in me to even the score for pa; but no man takes a life lightly if he's in his right mind, and I wasn't about to kill anybody unless they forced me to it. Besides, I'd put some miles behind me since I was the kid whose pa they'd hung. Though I was still nothing but a slim, tall boy, I'd met men and faced up to them before this, and I knew the kind of rabble I faced now.

Pelly strode up and banged his big fist on the door. "Open up, kid! I know you're in there!"

Softly I crept up the ladder to the loft. The cabin was built with an overhang so defenders could keep Indians from building fires against the log walls . . . that was back in the old days.

There was a plug right over where Pelly would be standing, a plug that stopped up a loophole. Easing it out, I looked down on Pelly, who was banging on the door again. Then I taken out my pistol and thrust the muzzle through the hole, aiming at the log wall beside Pelly. The bullet would miss him, but he would get a face full of slivers. I squeezed the trigger.

In the loft the gun boomed like a cannon. There was a startled cry, then a scramble of boots running, and I went down the ladder to the door. I peered through one loophole after another, but I saw nothing. All was dark and still. My unexpected shot had scared them off, but they would come back, twice as many and twice as mean.

Stud Pelly was a bragger and he would want to say he'd run me off. Well, he could say it, for I would be gone. When I came back again I would be a bigger, tougher, older man, and then I would have something to say to both Pelly and Brimstead.

Taking what was worth taking, I slid down the rope to the mule, and took off down the old Cherokee trails. And that time I was gone for a year.

At Independence I latched onto a freight outfit trailing west to Santa Fe. We had a couple of brushes with Indians, but nothing to amount to anything. In Santa Fe I hired out to a cattle outfit, worked a few months, then bought an outfit myself and went to hunting buffalo on the Staked Plains.

When I rode back to Tennessee again I was astride the dun, packing a Colt revolving shotgun, a .44 Henry, and a six-shooter.

The cabin was still standing, but the logs were scarred with bullets and the door had been broken down, then re-hung by somebody who was no hand with tools. The place had been swept out.

This time I wasn't staying. It was home-sickness that brought me back, or maybe it was just trouble-hunting, for being just past eighteen I was a far different person from the thirteen-year-old who had been forced to watch his father hung. I was pushing past six feet in height, and I weighed a solid one hundred and eighty pounds. I'd done my share of hard work and fighting, and on the buffalo ranges my shooting had been as good as the best. I wasn't ready to go hunting them, but if they came for me they'd buy themselves a packet of trouble.

Nobody came. It was quiet in the high-up hills. I went to sleep at night to the soft sound of the pines, awoke to drink good, cold spring water, and I worked a little around the place. Mostly I just stretched out on my back reading a pack of dime novels and magazines brought in from the outside. For two months I loafed and considered the future . . . whatever of a future I hoped to have.

That is, nobody came until the last day. There was a restlessness on me then, and a honing for far-off places. I'd cleaned my guns and was working over the leather of my gunbelt and holster when I suddenly decided to ride out for the West. My grub was about gone, so it was time to leave. I had started packing the last of my outfit when I heard a girl singing.

She was coming up along the creek that ran downhill to the Dunvegan place, and from the way she was singing I knew she was not expecting to see anybody. Then she stepped clear of the woods and pulled up short. It was Kitty Dunvegan.

It was Kit, only something had happened to her in the year I'd been away. She'd started showing quite a figure in all the proper places, and most of her freckles were gone, leaving only a sprinkling over her nose.

"Oh . . . it's you!" she said. Suddenly I was glad that I was cleaned up for travel, with a fresh shave and my hair combed and all. "I didn't think there'd be anybody here."

"I wasn't exactly notifying folks," I said.

"Have you been here long? I've been off to school." Her eyes went to my saddled-up horse. "You going away?"

"It came on me to ride. To Santa Fe, maybe, or somewhere north."

"It must be wonderful to just ride off . . . anywhere you want to, like that. Have you ever been to Santa Fe?"

"Yes, ma'am. I worked for a freight outfit going out. I rode for a cattle ranch south of there around Tularosa."

"Are the Spanish girls pretty?"

"I reckon so. Black eyes, and all."

"Do you like black eyes?"

"Until now," I said, looking into her blue eyes, "I always thought them the prettiest."

She blushed a mite, and it was fetching. So we just sat talking for a spell, of all manner of things, and I told her some about Indian fighting on the plains of the buffalo.

"Will you ever come back?" she asked.

"Nothing to come back for," I said. "I've been coming for the mountains and this ol' cabin. It ain't much, but it's mine. This Chancy land is deeded land, and I kept the taxes paid, and all. But I don't know if I'll ever come again . . . Maybe when I'm an old man."

"You could come to see me," she said.

"What would your sister say? And your friends down on the flatland?"

"I won't care. I won't care what anybody thinks."

"I'll come then," I told her. "I'll surely come."

She laughed suddenly. "You scared them," she said. "You scared them all that last time. Even Stud Pelly . . ."

"They came a-hunting it." I looked at her. "You the one who has been sweeping up inside?"

Her cheeks grew pink. "I wanted it to be clean when you came back. Besides, I come here sometimes when I want to be alone. Pa said it was all right."

"We're neighbors, like. Our deeded land fronts against yours at the bottom of the hill. Grandpa and pa, they filed on the whole ridge. The land ain't of much account, but pa wanted it. We claimed some, and bought some."

Kit got up suddenly. "I've got to go. Priss will come looking for me."

"Does she come up here?"

"Oh, no. I don't believe anyone knows of that path but you and me."

"Well, it ain't much of a path."

All of a sudden I felt awkward. I had no idea what to do, so I thrust out my hand. "Kit, I'm coming back," I said. "You can figure on it. I daren't come back until I can stand against them. All of them, if need be."

"Don't you be too long," she said.

She walked away to the edge of the woods beside the brook, then looked back. "Pa wonders why you never called on your kinfolk for help," she said. "Everybody knows the Sacketts. They're fighters."

"I never asked for help. I ain't likely to."

That was all we said. When she was gone I threw a leg over the dun and hunted my path down the trail.

I was going to come back, all right. I was going to come back and face up to Martin Brimstead and Stud Pelly. And then I'd go calling . . . I'd go calling on Kitty Dunvegan.

3

Under the low gray sky, under the swollen clouds, our cattle moved westward. The narrow trail led between thickets of blackjack brush mixed with sumac and tangled blackberry bushes, with here and there a clump of prickly pear.

It was a raw, rough land, brown and sad beneath the lowering sky. The wind worried my hatbrim, and my face was occasionally splashed by huge drops, seemingly out of nowhere.

Thunder muttered sullenly above the low hills, and lightning played across the sky. I had seen such storms before this, and the dun was not a nervous horse. I had more than a storm to think of, for I was riding among enemies.

Four days we moved westward, making eight miles the first day, then twelve, then six, and finally a mere five. The cattle were badly strung out, but they were easy enough to handle. There was little opportunity for straying, for the blackjack thickets were almost impenetrable for miles.

Needful as it was to keep a wary eye for trouble, my

thoughts kept straying. If we could get these cattle to market, I could pay my note and have several times a thousand dollars left over. With that amount of money, if I was to handle it right, I could soon be a well-off man.

It was in my mind to become rich and then return to the mountains and show them what a Chancy could do.

The saddle is a place for dreaming when there's hours of trail ahead, or when night-herding. And it came over me that to be rich was not enough. A man must win respect, and not the kind that can be bought with money or won with a gun. My pa always taught me that a man should strive to become somebody. He never made it himself, but that was nothing against him, because he tried. He just never held the right cards. With me it would be different.

I won't claim that I didn't think of being a big man in the eyes of that girl back yonder. Fact was, she occupied a good bit of my dreaming these days, though I'd little enough reason to think I mattered all that much.

We made camp that night alongside a slow-moving stream with blackberry bushes, cottonwoods, and persimmons all about. It was a good camp, with a fine meadow of grass and firewood a-plenty. But when I rode up to the fire they all stopped talking, as if they had plans they didn't want me to hear.

Dishing up my food, I sat down away from the lot of them, but before I sat down I swung my holster around between my legs where the butt would be right at my hand whilst eating.

"You ain't a very trusting man," Gates commented.

"I've had small reason. But don't forget one thing. You've got half your herd and a thousand dollars coming that you wouldn't have, had I shot any slower. I could have been cold under the grass back yonder.

"And let me say this," I added. "The drive isn't over. Not by a long shot. There's rough country ahead, and some mighty mean Indians. If we get the herd through without trouble we'll be lucky."

"Have you been through here before?" Gates asked.

"No, but I've been through Kansas, and I've talked with men who drove up the trail from Texas. You folks are going to need me—you're going to need all the help you can get."

They didn't like it much, but Noah Gates was a mite more pleasant for a while. Over coffee he dug at me with questions about the country to the west. Just south of our route was Arapaho country, with Cheyennes, Comanches, and Kiowas not far off. I didn't hold back when I told them of what lay ahead. With the buffalo herds almost gone, those Indians would be hunting beef, and they knew how to get it.

For the next two days we had good drives, with occasional flurries of rain. It was cold, wet, and miserable, but a sight better than some of the hot, dusty drives I remembered when the heat rising from the bodies of the cattle had been stifling.

The weather was hard on the older men. Being young and tough and no stranger to work, I did more than my share. Meanwhile, I made a book tally of my stock. A man unused to working cattle might have the idea they all look alike, but a good cattleman will soon know every steer in a herd. My brands tallied to seven hundred and thirty-three.

At the crossing of the Canadian we met our first Indians, a small party of Shawnees, living in buffalo-hide lodges. Three bucks mounted ponies and rode over to meet us. Turning the dun, I went out to them.

Now, a long time back the Cumberland was Shawnee country, and a few of them had drifted back there to live, so I knew some of their lingo, and of course I'd picked up sign language from the Cherokees.

It turned out I didn't need either one. The youngest of them spoke American. We did some palavering, but I had my eyes on a buckskin pony I saw tethered near their lodges. Even at that distance, I could see it wore a brand, which meant that it might be a good cow horse.

Anyway, I could see, plain enough, that it was a mighty fine horse.

When I greeted them in Shawnee they wanted to know where I was from, and when I told them, they got all excited. They knew the Cumberland, and we talked about it some, about the country and the hunting.

They had been a long time without meat, they said, and they asked could I let them have a beef. I told them that I'd swap . . . what did they have?

Well, they trotted out moccasins, buckskin jackets, and an old worn-out Kentucky rifle, and a few other things. Finally I told them I needed a horse. How about that old, broken-down buckskin?

At that, they blew up. The buckskin was not old, he was young. He was a fine horse, their best horse, and he was not to be traded.

So I changed the subject. They wanted beef, and I needed an extra horse. I rarely smoked, but I carried tobacco, and now I dug out my pouch, passed it around, then rolled a smoke for myself. Meanwhile, I talked about the Shawnees, and about how my folks had come into Shawnee country among the first white men—how they had traded, traveled, and hunted with the Shawnees. I made out as if I'd forgotten all about any trading.

Now, contrary to what folks have been led to believe, Indians are great talkers, and the old stories told by their people are fresh in their minds. We talked about how the Shawnees, once friends of the Cherokees, had been driven from the Cumberland by them, but that now they were friends once more.

The cattle drifted by, moving slowly, as always, pausing here and there to graze a bit, then moving on. Finally I swung my horse as if to join the herd, and again the Indians asked for beef.

"I'll swap a fat steer for that buckskin," I said.

They refused, and I started off, but one of them called after me: "Three steers!"

The horse was worth three steers to me because I

was already overworking the dun, and once we got out
on open grass we'd need three or four horses each to
handle those cattle. Even that number wouldn't be
enough to do the job really right. Moving through the
brush as we had been doing, there wasn't much chance
so far for the stock to stray.

We bargained for a spell, and the upshot of it was
that I got the buckskin for two steers. When I cut them
from the herd, Gates looked mighty sour. "If you don't
make good on that note," he said, "that buckskin be-
longs to us."

"What you'd better think about," I told him, "is how
much work he'll save you. I'm already doing as much
as any two of your crowd. The better horses I have to
ride, the less your men will have to do."

That made sense, and it shut him up, and the others,
too.

In all that while I'd exchanged no words with the redhead. Oh, she was a pretty one, all right, with a feisty
way about her, avoiding me, but never staying long out
of sight. She knew what she had, and she wanted to be
sure I knew it, too.

The thing was, she was avoiding me without any
need. I'd trouble enough, without giving them excuse to
shoot me. If they did shoot me, I was determined that I
wasn't going to make it easy for them.

The next morning we took the herd across the Canadian. It was low water, and we had to swim only a
short piece. Mostly it was just crossing a wide, sandy
wash. Now we were moving up onto the plains. The
grass was brown but there was plenty of it; and because
of the recent rains there were pools of water.

Noah Gates was riding point when I came up to him.
"The Chisholm Trail's not far ahead," I said to him.
"We can ride north for Abilene."

There were nine of us, and the girl. Or should I say
there were nine of them and one of me? For I stood
alone. I knew it and they knew it. I'd thought that may-

be I might win them over by hard work and doing more than my share, but their minds were closed against me.

I had come among them a stranger. I had bargained when they were desperate and afraid, and they hated me because I had not been afraid, and because their fear had driven them to surrender. But my willingness to fight had been my only stock in trade. It was all I had to sell, and had I been killed not one of them would have wasted a thought on me.

It worried me now to consider what lay before us. We were riding into Indian lands, and there's nobody quicker to spot weakness in a man than an Indian. A brave man might ride through the middle of an Indian band, where a frightened man wouldn't get twenty feet. And there wasn't much doubt that we were going to meet Indians.

It was almost noon when a brindle steer cut for the brush. I was riding the buckskin, which had proved to be a top cutting horse, and the buckskin went after that steer like a coyote after a jack rabbit. No matter which way he turned, the buckskin was right on him, so the steer headed back for the herd.

Pulling up on the edge of the brush, I started to reach for my tobacco. There was a clump of brush nearby, and some cottonwoods. I was lighting a smoke when I heard a low voice call from the brush. It was the redhead. She was standing beside a big cottonwood, her horse alongside. "Come over here," she said. "I want to talk to you."

Curious, I glanced around. The herd was grazing along, moving a few steps at a time. We'd come upon good grass, and Gates was letting them make their own pace. Turning my horse, I walked it over to where she stood.

"Get down. I have to talk to you."

Swinging down, I took off my hat and went up to her. She came even closer. She was an almighty pretty girl, with the kind of a body that could have made even some of those oldsters feel like a boy. But I didn't trust her.

"What's the matter?" she asked me. "Don't you even have time to talk to me?"

All of a sudden she threw both arms around me. Not around my neck, but around my arms, and even as she grabbed me, I heard a stir behind me, and as I struggled to throw her off, something crashed down on my skull. The next thing I knew I was on my face in the dusty grass and somebody was fumbling in my pockets.

"It ain't there, damn it!" someone said. The voice was not familiar.

I started to move, but it was the wrong thing, because whoever it was clobbered me again, and I heard the girl laugh.

The next thing I knew was the sound of rain falling on a hide tent, and the crackling of a fire. My eyes opened on a smoky firelight. I must have tried to move, for suddenly there was a face leaning over me, and I heard some muttered words in Shawnee. Then another face was there—this was the young Indian from whom I'd traded the buckskin.

"You feel better?" he asked.

"Where am I?"

"Near the Washita."

It came back to me then—the redhead grabbing my arms, and somebody—a young man by the sound of his voice—clobbering me.

"Where's my hat?" I asked.

I started to sit up, but pain hit me like a shot in the skull, and I fell back, holding my head with both hands.

The young Shawnee brought me a hat. "That's not mine," I told him.

"Pretty poor hat," he said. "Maybe somebody took yours?"

"You found me. What did the tracks look like?"

He squatted on his heels, chewing on a chunk of jerky. "A girl waited. You rode up and got down.

Somebody was behind a tree, waiting—he hit you—maybe two, three hours later we found you."

Carefully I sat up, my head swimming. I looked over at him. "Thanks," I said.

Grinning, he said, "Thank your hard head," and we both laughed.

"And you?" I said. "You are with the Shawnees, but your English is good."

"My full name is Jim Bigbear, and I am a full-blooded Indian. Trouble is, when I was only a boy I hired on with a cattle outfit as a horse wrangler. I've worked for cattle and freight outfits ever since, except one time when I scouted for the army for a few months. Anyway you look at it, I'm a maverick. I'm not a white man, but I don't fit in with the Indians any longer, either."

"You belong with me," I said. "We're cut from the same hide. . . . And now," I asked, "who was it hit me?"

Jim helped himself to my tobacco and answered my question. "One of the men who followed your herd. A young man who rides a black horse."

I contemplated that. No young men were with our outfit, nor any black horses. Jim had said one of the men who *followed* the herd, and I knew of no such men.

"Four men followed you," he went on. "At night one comes up close, and sometimes talks with the girl."

Evidently at one such meeting they had decided to steal my contract with the drovers.

Had they any connection with Noah Gates and his crowd? The more I considered the situation and their actions, the more I doubted it.

"You will go after them now?" Jim asked.

Then I explained to him about the cattle, and he listened with attention. "It seems to me you could use some help."

"I'd not turn it down if it comes, but I'd ask no man

to buy in with me. If there's trouble, it will be gun trouble."

"I've worked with cow ranches since I was knee-high," he said, "so whenever you're ready to ride . . ."

"We'll eat," I said, "then we'll go."

We took a pack horse and two spare mounts and made our start, riding steady and hard until noontime. Then he made coffee and swapped horses. A little short of sundown we shifted our saddles back to the original horses and rode on until midnight. By the time we rolled into our blankets it was safe to say we had covered as much ground in one day as the cattle would in four.

But there was no question about it. I was in no shape to ride. Three times I'd had to pause to throw up, and my head drummed all day long. Half the time I was only partly conscious, but I stayed in my saddle and kept moving.

On the second day we eased the pace a mite, but started early and took a two-hour break to let the horses graze on some good grass. By sundown we had gained two more days on the herd.

No sooner had we started on the third day than we saw the graves. They were fresh graves, and the names were familiar. Earl Williston had been the youngest of the crowd with our herd, and he had died here. Gene Brash I scarcely knew, but I remembered the name. There had been nine men and the girl. Now there were only seven left, and likely some of them were wounded.

Jim was scouting around. "Kiowas . . . eight or ten of them, and they ran off some stock. Twenty, twenty-five head."

"Will they go far?"

"Kiowas? Not on your life. They're not worried, so they'll ride off to camp by water and they'll roast some beef. They know the cattle drivers will need every man they've got to hold the cattle."

We trailed the Kiowas west about six, seven miles before we smelled smoke. The cattle were grazing on a small meadow, and the Kiowas had butchered a steer.

"I'll spook their horses. You go after the cattle."

We got close, for the Kiowas weren't expecting trouble—and they had their jaws full of meat. We cut loose with our six-shooters and stampeded horses and cattle right out of there. One Kiowa had a dead aim on me when Jim cut him down. We saw his rifle fly high, and then he hit the ground and rolled over.

Three miles north of there we rolled the stock into a tight bunch and looked them over. Eight of the cattle were mine. We also had four Indian ponies, having lost the others somewhere out on the grass.

We pushed on then, keeping the cattle to a steady trot for a couple of miles, then slowing them to a walk for a mile or more, and then to a trot again. They would be ga'nted up some, but we wanted to leave those Kiowas behind.

The four riders were still trailing our herd, and it was still about five days ahead. By the time we reached the Salt Fork we had gained two more days by almost running the legs off our stock.

Jim had been studying the tracks around the camps whenever we came to them, and he figured only five of the old men were able to ride, which meant that two wounded men must be riding the wagon.

The night after we swam the Salt Fork in flood. Jim squatted over the fire and sipped his coffee until I'd finished eating. "I think we have great trouble, *amigo*. I think I know the track of one of the horses of those who follow the herd—the horse and the rider as well. He is what they call a Bald Knobber . . . a bad man. His name is Andy Miller."

The name meant nothing to me but I'd not spent much time in this part of the country. "Is he the man on the black horse?"

"No. He rides what the Mexicans call a *grulla* . . . the color of a mouse. He has killed some men, that one."

This was pretty country seen at a sorry time. The blackjack leaves were crisp and brown, and they clung to the branches in spite of wind and rain. The trail was fresh, and we rode now with our guns loose in our holsters, momentarily expecting trouble.

My headaches had dulled, but towards evening they grew worse. But I was never inclined to coddle myself, and figured it was better to be up and doing.

We fought shy of cattle herds. Nearly every day we saw cattle, or the dust from moving herds. We held to low ground when we could, but the country was opening out around us, growing flatter as we went on, and concealment was impossible. This meant the four riders must stay even further back of the herd.

Abilene was not far away. We were closing in on the town, and that also meant the day would soon be here when we must face up to our trouble.

"You don't have to take cards," I said to Jim. "This here is my game."

He did not speak at all for a time, then he said, "You belong anywhere, Otis Tom?"

"I can't say that I do. I've got kinfolk around, but I never really met up with them. There's a girl I cotton to, but she's beyond me. That is, I've nothing to offer her. No, I can't say as I belong anywhere."

"Me neither."

We turned in after that, and after I'd been lying there a while, staring up at the stars and contemplating, I said to Jim, "Can you read?"

"Sure," he answered. "A Moravian missionary taught me. As a matter of fact, I've had eight years of good schooling."

Well, now. Somehow I'd never thought of an Indian reading, but then I recalled hearing that before Jackson and Van Buren moved them west the Cherokees even had their own newspapers, written in their own language, a language written out by Sequoyah. The Moravian missionaries had done good work among the Indians from the earliest times, and many of them were very intelligent folks.

This Indian, come to think of it, was the first friend

I'd ever had, and in a lifetime a man is lucky if he has one good friend.

He'd had a good bit more schooling than I had had, and more than likely from better teachers. Schooling for me meant riding over the mountain a-horseback, and I'd gone five or six years, but pa taught me a good bit at home, for he was something of a reader when he had time.

In those times there were a lot of educated men in the West, and many a night I've sat up in saloons or bunkhouses and listened to the talk of cities and of other countries, of wars and weapons, of writing men and of music, and of many other things.

I lay there thinking. If I could sell my cattle in Abilene and pay my note, I could buy some fine clothes and take time to read up on some of the things folks talked about; and then of an evening when men talked together, I might take part and put in a word or two. It was something to think on.

4

For fifteen miles before we got to Abilene we saw cattle all about us. They were well scattered, grazing on the good grass that was broken up here and there by fenced farms where crops were or had been planted. We counted maybe six to eight good-sized herds and half a dozen smaller ones.

On the farms there were corrals and lean-to barns, with sod houses for the most part; but here and there somebody had built a frame house out of shipped-in lumber. By some of the houses trees had been planted, and some had flowers around, but most of the places were bare-looking, and without any fixing.

Abilene itself wasn't much. The Drovers' Cottage was the first thing we noticed. A good hotel, with the best wines, whiskies, and cigars, it had been built by Joe McCoy. He'd had the foresight to see it all, to begin it all, and then he'd had the bad luck to lose most of it.

There was Henry's Land Office . . . the Metropolitan Hotel . . . both of them two-storied brick buildings, and across the street was a bank. Right beside the board-walk at Henry's Land Office was a well; so we pulled up there and looked the street over. Jim had himself a drink, and then I took one from the tin dipper.

"You think they're here?" he asked.

"Some of them will be holding the cattle, but the rest will be in town." I wiped my hand across my mouth. "I want to get my hat back."

"You take it easy," he said. "D'you know who's marshal here?"

"No."

"Bill Hickok . . . Wild Bill."

Everybody knew about Hickok. He was a tall, fine-looking man who had been a sharpshooter and a spy during the War Between the States, and he had worked for a stage line. He had killed Dave Tutt and a few others, and nobody who knew him underrated his skill with a gun.

If you came into town and minded your own affairs you had no trouble. Hickok, they said, was inclined to live and let live. But the idea was, just don't start anything, and above all, don't talk big about how good you were with a gun . . . and don't talk about treeing the town.

"I don't want trouble," I said, "least of all with him."

We cleaned up at the trough near the Twin Livery Stables, listening to Ed Gaylord talk. He was a friendly man, and nothing happened without his hearing of it.

"You ride in with a herd?" he asked.

"We came up the trail with one," I said, "but I got dry-gulched back down the line. I'm looking for the herd now—a man named Noah Gates is ramrodding it."

"They came in last night," Gaylord said.

Jim Bigbear was leading our horses back to a stall. Gaylord jerked his head at him. "Looks like an Indian."

"Shawnee," I said. "Used to scout for the army. A good cowhand and a damn good man."

"All right," Gaylord said mildly. "I only commented."

"I want folks to know," I said quietly. "He's with me."

"Are you somebody?" Gaylord studied me coolly. "Should I know you?"

"Mr. Gaylord," I said, "there's no reason why you should know me. If you ask if I'm good with a gun, I'll tell you honest, I'm as good as the next man. But I don't figure to make my way with a gun. I figure to buy and sell cattle, and maybe land. I say there's no reason why you should know me—but you give me five, ten years. Then you ask that question, and folks will think you're crazy."

He chuckled. "Well, you've told me, boy. And I kind of think that five or ten years from now I won't have to ask that question."

"Something more," I said. "I've got an interest in that herd Gates brought in. There's folks who'd like to horn-swoggle me out of it. But they aren't going to do it, and I'll handle it without guns if I can. I'm a peace-loving man, Mr. Gaylord. You remember that."

After that we went up the street together, Jim Bigbear and me, two tall young men, swinging along the boardwalk with a long, easy stride, our spurs a-jingling.

At the second bar we saw a black, beautiful horse outside, dusty from the trail. There was a mouse-colored horse tied alongside. "They're here," Jim said. "You want to face them?"

"No," I said, "he'll have his hat on. I'll wait."

There were plenty of folks around, and we stood together on the street, watching for somebody from the herd.

Abilene looked bleak and weather-beaten. Much of the town was still showing raw, unpainted lumber, but there was a sense of pride showing up, and folks were busy painting and planting, trying to make things look better.

The folks along the street looked to be from everywhere, lots of them foreigners—German, Scandinavian, and Polish, with a sprinkling of Britishers. Some of the people wore homespun, many wore jeans and chaps, but there were plenty of store-bought suits too, and some fine tailored clothes. Nobody liked his clothes creased in those days—that was the mark of the shelf, and the tailored suits were never creased.

Gamblers, cattle buyers, and local businessmen dressed mighty well, but even the cowhands in off the range put on their best, whatever it was. Nobody wore range clothes to town if he had anything else, unless he was working.

There were a few farmers in their wagons, usually with their wives and youngsters. Most of them wore flat-heeled boots and suspenders, and they didn't have much to do with the cowboys. The old honkytonks in Fisher's Addition had been closed, and the houses were licensed, like the saloons.

It was a lesson to a man just to stand there and watch folks go by; it was the well-dressed men to whom folks paid the most mind.

"How you figure to get your hat?" Jim asked.

"Why, I'll try to get it without trouble. But if they want trouble, they're going to get it."

He gave me a sharp glance. "You know how to use that gun?" He lit a cigarette. "If you aren't almighty good with it, you'd better not open the ball, believe me. Andy Miller is good, and chances are that man riding the black horse is just as good . . . maybe better."

"I can use it," I told him. "I don't know if I use it well enough. I guess I've got to pay to find out." Then I added, "If there's gunplay, they'll have to start it. But I've got an idea that I can pull it off without a fight."

"What do we do?"

"We wait. Meanwhile we scout around and try to locate the herd."

"Where were they going?" he asked. "Were they going to sell out here?"

It was a question I should have asked myself, for what had they to gain by selling in Abilene? I was the one who stood to gain by that; and for all they knew,

I might be dead. They might decide to sell out and call an end to it, but they might recapture their dream.

"They were talking of a green valley somewhere out west," I said. "A place folks had told them about."

Jim smiled. "Isn't that what we're all hunting for? A green valley somewhere?"

Suddenly I saw him coming down the street . . . Wild Bill himself. He was a tall, finely built man with a drooping mustache. He wore a black hat, a black, tailored suit, and a red sash with pistols thrust behind it. He was walking in our direction, and I faced him squarely.

He looked straight at me. I was a stranger, but there was no wariness in his eyes, only that cool attention he gave every man. I knew he was good. You could feel it.

"Mr. Hickok?" I said.

"Yes?"

"Mr. Hickok, I'm Otis Tom Chancy. I'd like to talk to you for a minute."

He glanced from me to Jim Bigbear. "Howdy Jim," he said quietly. "This man a friend of yours?"

"Yes, he is."

He turned back to me. "What is it, then?"

Briefly, I explained about the bill of sale for the herd, how I'd been slugged, and my hat taken. I told him who the man was who'd done it, and about Andy Miller. And then I told him how I hoped to get my hat back.

He listened, watching me carefully all the while. Then he said, "Why tell me all this?"

"Because this is your town. You keep the peace here, and I'm a man who respects the law. If the man who did it wants trouble he can have it, outside of town. I wanted you to know I wasn't hunting trouble. But I want my hat back, and what's in it."

"Have you any proof the hat is yours?"

So I explained about that, and about the bill of sale. "All right," he said finally. "I'll be around."

After he had walked on up the street, I looked at Jim. "You didn't tell me you knew him," I said.

"Didn't figure it mattered. We were scouts for the army at the same time, a few years back. He's a good man."

And just then I saw them.

Three men came out of a saloon together: a short, thickset man with his vest torn in the back; a slender, wiry man with a still, cold face, reddish hair, and a few freckles; and a third one—tall, and good-looking in a rakish, hell-for-leather sort of way. And this one wore my hat.

Jim Bigbear straightened up, blocking my view. "Don't look at them," he said. "That's Caxton Kelsey."

Well, I didn't know the names of many folks in this part of the country, but I'd heard tell of Caxton Kelsey on my way to Santa Fe, and since. He was a gunfighter, and by all accounts a holy terror. He'd killed six or seven men that folks knew of, and he was accounted a bad man to tangle with.

So I just stood still there, giving it some thought. I had used guns since I was old enough to hold one level and take aim, but I'd never considered myself a gunfighter or anything of the sort. I'd been around, I'd shot rifles at Indians when they attacked our freight outfits, but so far as I knew the only man I'd ever killed was that would-be sheriff back in the Territory. And I was smart enough to know I didn't qualify to hold a gun against Caxton Kelsey.

But I wasn't about to give up all I'd lose if I didn't get my hat back. I didn't know what was between him and that redhead, and it was none of my affair. I just wanted my hat.

Now, there's more than one way of doing things, and when a body can't come about it one way, he can do it another. Of course, the way I was thinking of might lead to shooting. All I could do was play my hand and keep my chips in the pot.

We stood there, seeming to pay them no mind, and soon they crossed the street to an eating place. We watched them go in, hang up their hats, and sit down, and then I led the way across the street. As I did so, I saw Bill Hickok take the cigar from his mouth, flip off the ashes, and follow us.

They were paying no attention when we came in, and I hung Kelsey's hat that I'd been wearing on a hook right alongside my own black one that he'd had. Then we sat down close by, and a moment later Hickok came in and crossed the room to a seat near the wall.

We ordered coffee. We'd been sitting there maybe three or four minutes before Andy Miller happened to look around and see me. He leaned over and whispered something to Caxton Kelsey, who lifted his eyes and looked right at me and smiled.

Yes, sir. He just looked at me and smiled, as much as to say: *Well, here I am. What are you going to do about it?*

I just grinned back at him. "I've still got a sore head," I said to him.

He was startled. I don't think he expected that, or anything like it. He shrugged and said, "Don't let it get you into trouble."

"I'm not likely to. I'm a peace-loving man myself."

I put two-bits on the table to pay for the coffee, and got up. "So much so that I'm going to leave you boys to eat in peace. Come on, Jim."

Stepping over to the hatrack, I took down my black hat—my own hat.

Kelsey sat up straight. "You've got the wrong hat, *amigo*. That's mine."

"You had the wrong one," I said, still with a grin. "You just picked up the wrong hat back on the prairie. Now you've got your own back."

He did not move, but he said in a quiet voice, "Put it down, kid. Put it down while you've got a chance."

"What seems to be the trouble, gentlemen?" That was Bill Hickok.

Now, I didn't for a moment figure that Caxton Kelsey was afraid of Hickok. He'd taken his own share of scalps, and he was a good man with a gun, but Hickok was standing about twenty feet back of Kelsey's right shoulder. Jim and me were about ten feet apart, and facing him.

He was boxed neatly, but he was a warrior, and he knew when he was out of position.

Before he had a chance to speak, and maybe make an issue of it that none of us could get out of, I said, "This is my hat, Marshal. It's got my initials inside."

They were there, all right, but stamped so small they could hardly be seen, and the chances were he had not noticed them. Holding the hat, my fingers had already found the bill of sale. Even if I lost the hat, I was going to keep that.

There were half a dozen other men in the restaurant, and I handed the hat to the nearest one without taking my eyes off Kelsey. "My name is Otis Tom Chancy," I said. "You'll find my initials in the hatband right along the bow in the back of the sweat-band."

The man took the hat and looked inside. "That's right," he said. "OTC . . . right on the sweat-band."

Hickok said, "I think that settles it, gentlemen. Shall we all relax now?"

Well, I put on my hat but, boylike, I couldn't resist having my say. As I put it on I said, "I'm glad to have this back. I left a bill of sale stuck behind the hatband."

Well, for a moment there I thought Kelsey was going to go for his gun. His face turned ugly and he made a half-move to rise. Then Hickok said, "Chancy, your horse is in the livery stable. You'd better get it."

"Yes, sir. Thank you, Marshal."

We stepped out on the walk, and we didn't waste any time heading for the stable. Jim stood in the doorway while I saddled up, and then I took over while he threw the leather on his mount. We gathered up our other stock and headed out of town.

It wasn't until Abilene was just a row of buildings on the horizon that Jim spoke. "You push your luck, cowboy," he said.

"Well," I said, "it was my hat, and those are my cows."

"He'll hunt you. He'll come looking for you."

I was packing my Colt shotgun across my saddle-bows, and had my rifle in the boot, close at hand. I was no match for Caxton Kelsey with a six-gun, and I knew it.

At the second herd we visited they told us where we could find Noah Gates.

We rode up to the wagon about sundown. Well, you should have seen their faces. They had given me up for dead, and here I was. Maybe the most surprised of them all was that redhead.

"Figured you was dead," Gates said. He glanced from me to Jim. "What happened?"

"That redhead over yonder," I said. "She's got herself a man. She set a trap for me and he laid me out with a gun barrel."

"He lies!" she said sharply. Her face didn't look so pretty right then. Fact is, I never saw so much hatred in a body's face. If somebody does you dirt and gets caught at it, they hate you all the more.

"Jim found me, or else I might have died," I said. "Then I had to trace her friend down and get my hat back."

"I don't believe you." Gates's skin was mottled and his eyes were downright mean as he spoke. "Queenie's my daughter-in-law. She wouldn't do such a thing."

"This man followed your herd all the way from the Nation, maybe further," I went on. "Jim and his Shawnee friends came on their tracks and studied them out. Your Queenie used to slip out of camp of a night and meet this man. I figure she told him about our deal, because he was hunting for that bill of sale. He never found it."

"Dad," Queenie said, "every word he says is a lie. He's no good, and the sooner we get shut of him, the better."

"The man's name is Caxton Kelsey," I said, "and

unless I'm mistaken he'll be riding out of Abilene, a-hunting me."

The name did it. Noah Gates knew that name, all right, and evidently he had cause for not liking it, because he turned sharp around on Queenie. "You took up with that murderin' no-account!"

"He's lying!" she repeated, but nobody was believing her any more.

"Then all you told us back in Texas was a lie. It was your fault back there," Gates said.

"Believe whatever you're of a mind to." She stood with her hands on her hips, contempt in every line of her. "Adam Gates was never much of a man, no matter what you thought of your precious son. He was never anything but just a big, awkward farm boy."

"You married him. You told him you loved him," Gates said.

"My folks were dead and I had nowhere to go—until Cax came along."

"He murdered my son . . . and you lied about it."

She shrugged. "Cax threw the gun down. He told Adam to pick it up, or get out and leave me with him. Adam was always a fool, so he reached for the gun."

If there was any feeling for the man she had married, it surely didn't show. I had a picture of Caxton Kelsey standing there waiting for that boy to pick up the gun . . . Kelsey just standing there, knowing how easy it was going to be . . . then shooting him down before he'd more than laid a hand on the gun.

"You'd better get out of here," the girl said, "unless you want the same. Cax is coming for me, and he wants the cattle. He's got Andy Miller and his brother Rad, and he's got LaSalle Prince."

Noah Gates stood there with empty hands, his thin shoulders sagging. Two of their men were dead, two more lay on their backs, too hurt to fight. Five men remained—five tired, worn-down men, none of them gunfighters. Even a dozen of them would have been no match for the gunmen she had mentioned. LaSalle

Prince was a notorious badman out of Missouri who had come into the feuds of eastern Texas, a cold-blooded killer, with a leaning toward the ambush or the surprise shooting.

"We've reached Abilene," I said. "I'm going to sell my cattle."

They stood silent, their faces stubborn against me, but in their eyes was the doubt and fear left by what Queenie had told them. They were thinking of Caxton Kelsey coming against them with his men.

I was giving that some thought, too, and mean as these fools had acted against me, I wished them no harm. I did not know the full story, but from what Queenie and Noah Gates had said, it seemed clear that she must have been carrying on with Kelsey, and when Adam Gates had come upon them Kelsey had killed him, with her standing by.

"Whatever you figure to do," I told them, "you'd best be planning. I've a notion that Kelsey is a fast-acting man."

"We can ride into town and get Hickok," Bowers suggested.

"He won't leave town," I said. "His job is keeping peace in the streets of Abilene."

Queenie was staring at me, her eyes filled with meanness. "He'll kill you," she said, "and I'll stand by to see it."

"There was a man back in the Nation who had the same idea," I said, "and he sleeps in a mighty cold bed tonight."

Gates had no idea what to do. You can't just up and run with a herd of cattle. They leave too wide a trail, and they are too slow. "He won't dare," he said finally. "We're too close in to a town. Folks wouldn't stand for it."

"Maybe so," I said. "It's your gamble."

They stared at me then. "What about you?" Gates asked. "You've got a stake in this."

"We're going to cut out our cattle, and we're going to sell . . . part of them, anyway."

"And the others?"

"Maybe we'll try for that green valley out yonder."

"What if they come up to you—just the two of you?"

"We'll fight," I said coolly, "and that's what I'd advise you to do. The first thing I'd do would be to tie up that—"

But she was gone.

She had been standing near the wagon, but she must have slipped behind it, and from there she had ducked into a draw where she'd had her pony tied.

"She'd figured on it all along," Gates said.

"She's going to meet him," I said, "and you can bet they'll come back here."

"What'll we do?" Gates was asking himself that question as much as anybody else, but I answered him.

"You've got a choice. You can stay here and wait and fight, or you can try running. If you stay, the thing to do is have only one man in the open. Give your wounded men rifles, and let a couple more get into the wagon, too. Then the rest of you get down out of sight, and when they come up, cut them down."

"We can't do that."

"Then you've got to run. Look," I went on, "the Half-Circle X moved their herd this afternoon. You can start off, lose your tracks in theirs. It won't keep them off you long, but you can buy yourself some time."

"And you?"

"We'll cut out our bunch and pull out. You lend us one man to help. You'll want somebody to pick up your money after we make our sale, anyway. That way Kelsey might follow us, or he might follow you."

There was nothing very good about the plan, but it was the best I could think of. There had been a lot of cattle moving over the grass, and following one herd wouldn't be too easy. And not even Caxton Kelsey would be wanting to bust into a strange Texas herd and get himself shot at in hunting for us.

Ordinarily we couldn't have done it in twice the time, but I'd noticed that a good many of our brands were grazing on the slope of the draw, and all I wanted at this point was a hundred head or so. If I could get that many into town and sell them, I could pay off for the herd. The rest would be so much gravy.

Reluctantly, Gates agreed, and even as he spoke, Jim was already moving. We rounded up about a hundred and fifty head and started them over the grass. We went due north and away from town, and drove the cattle down into a draw that curved around toward the bed of the Smoky Hill River.

We saw scattered cattle and a few cowhands rounding them up and pushing them back into the herd, but nothing else. We bunched the cattle in a hollow of the hills and, leaving Jim and the old man to hold them, I skirted the town and rode to the Drovers' Cottage.

Most of the cattle buyers were in the saloon. There were a lot of cattle around Abilene that year, and I wasn't expecting top prices. The stock we had cut out were mostly fat steers, in better shape than those that had been driven over the Chisholm Trail, and in much better shape than stock held on the prairies around Abilene. It had been a stormy year, cold and wet much of the time, and the grass had grown coarse and washed out. To the east it was much richer, and our stock had moved slowly for the greater part of the drive.

The bartender at the Drovers' directed me to Bob Tarlton, a tall, well-setup man in his late thirties. He was cool, handsome, and business-like. Briefly, I explained about my steers, how they had come up the Shawnee Trail where the grass was excellent and where there was no end of water.

He heard me out, and then said, "You understand there's no shortage of cattle? The market is glutted. You'd be well advised to drive north or west, and graze your stock until the market is better."

So I put my cards on the table, and he listened, smoking his cigar and looking out the window as I talked. I told him about the trouble in the Nation, and why I had to pay off right then. When I finished he turned around, gave me a straight, measuring look, and said, "Let's ride out and have a look."

When he stepped into the saddle he was packing a six-shooter and carrying a Winchester. He rode well, and there was no nonsense about the man. He rode around the cattle and through them, and he could see I'd told him true, that the stock was in good shape.

"All right," he said. "I make it a hundred and forty-two head. Is that about right?"

"I haven't counted them," I said frankly, "but that's about what I'd say."

"I'll give you sixteen dollars a head, and take delivery at the stockyards in Abilene."

"It's a deal." I thrust out my hand, and he took it.

He lit a cigar. "Your name is Chancy? What are your plans?"

"Well," I said, "I've got some working capital now. And I still own five, six hundred head of mixed stuff. I figured to move west, find myself a place of my own, and go to ranching."

"Have you thought about Wyoming? It's a good country, and there's water and grass."

I rode up to Jim and said, "All right, let's roll 'em."

Jim skirted the cattle, bunching them up and starting them moving. I rode point with Tarlton.

"It's a beautiful country," he said, "and if you were so inclined we might discuss a partnership. If you're going to ranch, you'll need capital."

There was sense in that, but somehow the idea of partner had not occurred to me. I was used to going it alone, and I told him so.

"Frankly, that's what I like about you," he said. "Ranching in this western country needs a man who can make decisions. You say you've got better than five hundred head. Well, prices on cattle are down right now, so suppose we figure your cattle at twenty dollars a head? That figures you'll be coming in with a capital of ten thousand dollars and your work. I'll match it with ten thousand and agree to contribute five hundred head of good breeding stock within the year. You'll make the drive west, find the land, build whatever we need."

There it was, laid out for me. It was the kind of chance a young man rarely got, and I'd done too little to earn it, it seemed to me.

"You don't know anything about me," I told him.

"I know enough." He glanced over at me. "News travels fast in this country. We'd heard about the shooting back in Indian country before you ever got here, and before you mentioned a word of it to me.

"Hickok told me about how you came to him with the hat story. He liked it, and so did I. It showed you had respect for the law, and how you would use your brains to save a fight if you could. Your cattle are in good shape, and I think you're just the partner I want."

We rode on into town and turned the cattle in at the stockpens. Then we went to the bank together and I collected my money and paid over the thousand dollars to the old man. "You tell Noah Gates I'll be coming after the rest of my cattle," I said. "I am going ranching in the western lands."

Jim and I squatted on our heels along the stockpens and talked it out. "I'll need you, Jim," I said, "and I'd like to have you along. I figure you could take up some land close by, and work for Tarlton and me until you get going with a spread of your own. Fact is, I'll start you with a few head and you can register your own brand."

"Have you forgotten Caxton Kelsey?"

"Not even a little bit. That's a bronc I've got to ride when the time comes. Meanwhile," I said, "I'm not going to let worry over him rule my life. It seems to me that if a man is going to get anywhere in this life, he'd better start for somewhere, and have something definite in mind."

"Do you know Wyoming?"

"No, but I've heard talk of it. One of the teamsters with a freight outfit I drove for soldiered up thataway, and had a lot to say about it. He was in the Wagon-Box Fight up yonder on the Bozeman Trail."

"You'll need some hands."

"I figure half a dozen good men. You keep your eyes open, and I'll do the same. I want men who savvy cattle, but who are willing to fight if need be."

"Well," Jim said dryly, "most of the broke cowhands around Abilene are from Texas and they cut their teeth on six-shooter steel."

In the Drovers' Cottage that evening over supper we drew up the papers, such as they were. A handshake would have done for either of us, but if anything happened to Tarlton he wanted it clear and clean for his heirs, back east.

Over coffee I told him about my plans for an education. "You'd be wise," he agreed. "It's a growing land, and an educated man with some drive can go far."

It was pushing midnight when I left the Drovers' and went out to the hitching rail. All was dark and still. Mounting up, I walked my horse up the street toward the Twin Livery Stable and rode in under the lantern that overhung the wide door.

Lights still shone from the doors of several places—the Alamo, the Bull's Head, Downey's, and Flynn's, among others. Stripping the saddle from the buckskin, I tied him to the manger in a stall, put some corn in the box, and slung my Winchester muzzle-down from my shoulder by its sling. Not many western men used the sling, but I did, and I'd found that a man could swing a rifle into action from the shoulder, in that position, as swiftly as a man could draw. The rifle butt was just about level with the top of my shoulder, my hand on the action of the rifle.

A man came out of a saloon up the street and staggered off. Somewhere I heard a door slam, and there was the tin-panny sound of a music box at the Alamo.

My boots made no sound in the dust as I went along,

for I had not reached the boardwalk. Now, I am by nature a cautious man, inclined not to trust appearances, whether in man or nature, and for a man with enemies that street was an almighty quiet place.

When I reached the shadow beside the first building, I stopped, giving study to the street ahead, and especially to dark doorways and alleys. I had no reason for suspicion beyond the fact that for a man with my enemies it would be wise to be watchful. And I'd never gone along a dark street in my life without being wary. So I stood there just waiting, watching to see who was going to move . . . if anybody.

Several minutes passed and all remained quiet, so I started on up the street, my boots now making echoing sounds on the walk.

Suddenly I saw a man standing half in the shadows, about fifty feet from the nearest lights. He was facing me. I could see the vague light on the side of his hat, a mite of his chin, and the gleam on the butt of his gun.

For the space of perhaps a minute we stood there, each of us half in darkness, half in shadow not quite so dark, each aware of the other, each poised for movement.

Up the street the sound of the tin-panny piano stopped, and there was a tinkle of broken glass.

"What's the matter, mountain boy?" The man's voice was low, unfamiliar. "Are you scared?"

5

Curiously enough, I was not scared. I was not even worried. I could see his gun hand and the butt of his gun. He could not move without my knowing it, so I just waited. I did not speak.

I'd taken to carrying my gun on the left side for a cross-draw, and that meant he could see my gun, too. What he couldn't see was the rifle, but even if he had he would not have worried, because nobody carried a rifle the way I did, and it looked as if it would be slow to use.

My silence seemed to make him uneasy, but if there was to be any shooting he was going to have to open the ball. I wanted no trouble in Hickok's town. He had played fair with me, and I intended to do the same.

"I'm going to kill you, mountain boy," came that voice again. "I'm going to put you down under the grass. I'm going to save Kelsey the trouble."

Across the street from me a match flared, lighting a cigar. The voice that spoke there was clear. "Rad Miller, you get your pony and ride out of town, and don't let me find you here again this year. I don't like trouble-hunters."

Miller hesitated only a moment, and then he walked toward me, and on past, muttering as he did so, "You'll get it. He can't protect you all the time."

Hickok's voice across the street said, "Obliged, Chancy. I don't want gun fights in Abilene. Can I buy you a drink?"

We walked into the Alamo together and stood at the bar. When we had our drinks, he brushed the ashes from his cigar and, glancing at my Winchester, said, "Odd way to carry a rifle." He looked at me thoughtfully from cold gray eyes. "You'd have killed him, Chancy."

"Maybe."

"No maybe . . . you'd have done it. You're one of the good ones. I can spot 'em a mile off." Then he said, "You staying around town?"

"No. I've made a deal with Tarlton. I'm going west to ranch in Wyoming."

"Good country. I'm going out to the Black Hills one of these days."

We talked idly of Indians and buffalo, of stage driving and of Custer, whom he knew. I told him about my plans with Tarlton, and said that I'd need some hands.

"There's a man here from Illinois," Hickok said, "his brother was in the army with me. He's hunting a job."

"Can he shoot?"

"Yes . . . and he can handle horses and cattle. His name is Tom Hacker. As a boy he was a blacksmith's helper, and later a smith himself. He rode with the cavalry for six or seven years."

"Send him to me. He sounds like just what we'll need."

Hickok left me and went along, making his rounds. I stood watching a poker game, and then I went back to the hotel. When I went in, a stocky, well-setup man with leather-like skin and mild brown eyes was there waiting for me. With him was a wiry, narrow-hipped fellow of about my own age.

"Mr. Chancy?" the older man said. "I'm Tom Hacker. This here is my nephew, Cotton Madden. We're rustling for work."

"All right. We're riding out in the morning to join the herd. You need any money?"

"No, sir. I've still got a few dollars." He grinned. "I'll be broke in the morning, though."

I went up to my room. It wasn't much, but it looked good to me. It was a front room looking out over the street, with a second window that looked on a small alleyway that separated the hotel from the building next door. There was a bed and a chair, and a washstand with a pitcher of water, a bar of soap, and a towel.

First thing, I pulled off my boots and put them beside the bed, then took off my shirt. I stood my rifle beside the washstand, and put my pistol on the bed, butt toward me. After I'd washed and combed my hair, I pulled off my pants and stretched out on the bed.

For the first time in days I was alone, with time to think. And for the first time in my life I had a definite goal. I had a partner, and I was going to take the herd west and locate a ranch. I had more money than I'd ever had in my life. And if I had the brains and the nerve to take advantage of my opportunity, I had a future.

Nothing about it would be easy. That country was still Indian country, and the white men who had drifted in there were mostly the lawless kind, ready for any kind of trouble. While I lay there stretched out on my back, I began to contemplate.

First, a corral. Then a dugout or a cabin, whichever seemed quickest and best . . . or if the weather was right we could start right away on a bunkhouse. I'd have to define my range, hunt a good bit to help out with the grub, and put up some hay for winter feeding. I'd have to build a shelter for my saddle stock . . . split logs, maybe, or poles, depending on what was to hand.

When I got up from the bed I belted on my six-gun and then put in almost an hour practicing the draw, both the cross-draw and a draw from the waistband. No getting around it, I was slower than I had any right to be, but there was nothing slow about the way I could get off a shot with my Winchester slung from my shoulder.

Finally, tired out, I stretched out on the bed again and slept.

When I came down the stairs in the freshness of morning, Jim Bigbear, Tom Hacker, and Cotton Madden were waiting for me. It was scarcely past daybreak, but the town was already alive and moving. We went into the restaurant, and a few minutes later Tarlton came in, another man with him.

This was a tall man with a drooping auburn mustache. He was so thin he would have had to stand twice in the same place to make a shadow. But he wore a six-gun as if he knew what it was for, and he carried a Winchester as if he was born to it.

"Chancy, this is Handy Corbin," Tarlton said. "You'll find him a good man."

Tarlton had brought along the last two mule loads of grub we were packing west, and within the hour we had headed out along the Smoky Hill River.

Busy as I'd been, I had been giving some thought to that red-headed woman, and also to the Millers and Caxton Kelsey. They wanted that herd, and they didn't size up to be the sort who would tuck their tails and run at the least thing.

When we rode up to the herd Noah Gates was the only one in sight. He glanced from me to the riders following, and he asked, "You come for the rest of your cows?"

"Uh-huh." I hung one knee around the saddle horn. "What are you figuring on doing, Mr. Gates?" I asked.

When they saw we were acting friendly, the others began to appear. My boys had scattered out a little, putting themselves in good shape for a fight if need be

—a fight with the oldsters, or with Kelsey if he showed up.

Gates chewed on his mustache. "We ain't decided. Some of us want to sell out here and now, but some want to drive on west, hunting for that green valley yonder."

"You've got about fifty head of yearlings in there," I said. "I'll buy them off you . . . five dollars a head, cash on the line."

"Five dollars? I hear tell you got sixteen."

"Maybe so . . . but they were full-grown steers. You won't get far selling yearlings—there's a glut on the market of everything right now. I want some breeding stock."

The upshot of it was that I made myself a deal . . . at six dollars a head, and it was good young stuff that I bought. We cut out the best of them, strong enough to stand the drive west—and the winter to follow, I hoped.

Over the fire Noah Gates told us the story about Queenie. She had come out from town, riding alone, and she had made an offer for the herd, a very small offer. When they refused to sell, she had threatened them. Gates had profited by my advice and they had forted up, and had done a better job than I'd expected, for they had gone back to the edge of the brush near a buffalo wallow and had dug sod to build a parapet.

Kelsey had ridden out and they had been ready for him. After a warning and one look around, Kelsey had ridden away.

"Ran 'em off, we did," Bowers said, excitedly. "They taken one look, and then they lit a shuck."

"So now what do you do?"

"We're pullin' out. We're goin' to take the herd west, like we planned. We've got money enough. We'll buy supplies, and then we'll head for Wyoming, like you're doin'."

"You think you've lost Kelsey?" I asked.

"You jokin'? Of course we've lost him. All he needed was a show of force. They won't come back."

"Not when you're out on the plains? With no fort?"

They exchanged a glance, then shrugged. "We'll gamble on it. Anyway, we're going to armor our chuck wagon. Double plank sides, with a couple of seasoned steer hides between the walls. We'll keep a couple of men ridin' the wagon with rifles."

We drank their coffee, cut our cattle out of the herd, and moved off. It needed only a few minutes to see that I had some hands who knew how to handle cattle. We drove due north, right out across the grass, and we pushed them hard for about eight or ten miles. When we bedded them down we were on a small creek where there was good water and grass.

"Jim, you take the first guard," I said. "I doubt if they'll find us this soon, so you'll be all right alone. Tom, you and Cotton take the second trick. I'll take the graveyard trick with Corbin."

The night passed quietly, and by sunup we were on the trail again. Jim helped start the cattle, then he rode off down our backtrail.

Handy Corbin pulled up beside me on the drag. "That Injun good on the trackin'?"

"The best I ever saw."

He glanced at my six-gun. "Are you any good with that?" he asked.

"I never had a chance to find out. I can put them where I want them, but I wouldn't rate as a really fast man."

"Don't try for that, then. Just get it out, no matter what, and make the first one count. Hell," he added, "half the fast men waste their first shot, anyway."

We rode on for half a mile or so, and then Corbin said, "You can leave it to me—the gun-fightin', I mean."

"You're that good?"

"Well," he answered with a grin, "I'm still alive."

Nobody was going to do my fighting for me; nonetheless I welcomed the feeling that this man stood ready and willing. There was no need to tell him I'd handle it. I've seen that circumstances have a way of dictating conditions, so that few men have any choice when the chips are down.

We had nigh onto six hundred head of cattle, mostly young stuff, but all of it was trail broke. I didn't have to do more than my share, for these men were all young. Tom Hacker was the oldest . . . he was close to thirty. Handy Corbin was twenty-seven or -eight. They all knew cattle, and they were always ready to do their part, and a bit more.

The route we were taking was on the north side of the Smoky Hill River, and parallel to it. The grass was good, and we watered at streams that would flow into the Smoky Hill, or sometimes at ones that would flow into the Republican River or some other river to the north. I never had been up into that part of the country, so it was mostly hearsay with me. The only difference the streams made was that some were fresh and some were alkali.

In three days we made thirty-two miles, we figured. After the first day, we took it easy, and after that day we were driving over virgin grass. Once we saw a few buffalo in a grassy bottom, but on sighting us they had taken off, and we didn't give chase.

Cotton killed three wild turkeys on the third day out, so we had a change from the usual grub. That night it was windy and chilly, and there were coyotes around. Jim was restless, and a little short of sundown he mounted up and rode out. Hacker watched him go.

"There's a good Indian," he said. "You known him long?"

"Long enough," I answered. "He'll do to ride the river with."

Jim came back in time to take first guard, and I stood part of it with him, for I was some restless myself. We'd been lucky so far, but I had no faith in that, never being one to depend on luck. I knew Jim felt the same way, and maybe the others did. Tom Hacker and Cotton had their watch, and then it was Corbin's and my turn.

But when the night showed itself to be quiet, I had sent Corbin in to get some sleep. I had a feeling we were going to need all the rest we could get. I stood watch alone for the last two hours. When the stars were fading I came into camp to stir the fire into life and put on the coffeepot.

The truth of the matter was that I liked being alone out there in the early morning. I liked seeing the night pale and the stars wink out one by one, like candles snuffed by a quiet wind. I liked seeing the pink color the east and the dark trees begin to take on shape. At times like this I felt the way the Indians must have felt, for this was a country to be alone in—a broad, beautiful land with the grass bending to the faint stirring of wind, and the steers rising from the ground, humping their backs to stretch out the stiffness of night, looking around and beginning to crop grass a little.

I liked the sound of the grass being cropped, and thought this was a fine land to rear children in, to see a man's sons grow tall, breathing deep of the fresh air, drinking cold stream water, and smelling bacon frying.

Out there, I heard a stirring in the brush, and the cattle looked up, ears pricked, wary against danger. I spoke to them softly, walking my horse through them toward the sound, and then the brush parted and up from the stream came a huge old buffalo bull, his great head shaggy and wild. He stood for a minute, trying the wind and looking at us, but I held the buckskin still, not wanting to spook the old fellow, who looked to have had trouble enough in his time.

After a moment he walked on, his big head swaying to his step, and then from the brush came a cow and a yearling, and they followed him across the clearing and out of the valley.

"Go ahead, old fellow," I said. "We could use the meat, but you belong to this place more than I do, so go along, and the best of luck to you."

They walked solemnly ahead, seeming to guess that I held no designs against them.

The cattle were up and day had come while I watched. A bird was twittering in the bushes nearby, and I saw the bright crimson of a cardinal as it flitted off.

Swinging my horse, I had started toward camp when I glanced once more toward the buffalo. They were up on the low hill that bordered the basin where we had camped and bedded the herd, and they had stopped there, heads up, peering off toward the west. As I looked, they suddenly tossed their heads and turned, trotting off toward the east.

My rifle slid into my hand and I walked the buckskin toward the place where the buffalo had been. There I slid from the saddle, trailing the bridle reins. My boots made hardly a sound in the grass, only the faintest of whispers. At the crest of the hill I flattened out, and eased my head up beside a clump of butterfly bush.

I saw a man out there, staggering roughly in my direction. As I looked, he fell, lay still a moment, and then heaved himself up and came on. His shirt was bloody and he looked about gone; there was a familiar way about him that made me come to my feet. Then he fell again, and a rider came over the hill.

The rider had not seen me. He came on down with his rifle ready, and it was plain to see that he meant to kill the wounded man. I started toward them, walking carefully. The wounded man was closer to me than to the other man. When the killer was about thirty yards off, the wounded man tried to rise up.

"Leave me be!" he shouted hoarsely. "Leave me be, damn you!"

The rider drew up and lifted his rifle. "You're the last of them, old man, an' I'm going to cut you down. I'm going to make buzzard bait of you."

"Hello, Rad," I said, and he turned as if he'd been stabbed.

I walked a couple of steps toward him. "Rad, you

said Wild Bill was protecting me in Abilene. Well, there's no Wild Bill around now. Just you, me, and that old man you're itchin' to kill."

He didn't like it. He'd figured me for a yellow-belly, a tenderfoot that he could take without trouble; but now I was ready, asking for it, and it bothered him.

The old man on the ground had lost his gun, and was unarmed. It was just between Rad and me.

"What's the matter, Rad?" I said. "You just like killing old men? Are you afraid to tackle a full-grown man in broad daylight?"

Oh, he didn't like it—he didn't like it a-tall. I'd come up within about twenty-five yards of him now, almost abreast of him and on his right side. Now, it's a mighty easy thing to swing a rifle to cover your left, but sitting a horse when you have to bring it around to your right, it's slow . . . and he knew it.

He was starting to sweat, but I had no feeling of mercy for him. If he had me in that spot he'd have killed me as quick as he'd wink, and he had surely intended to kill that wounded man.

"You boys opened the ball," I said, "now you can dance to the music."

Deliberately, I was baiting him. This was a chance to lower the odds against us, so I took a step forward, moving a little farther into range. He thought he had me then, and he whipped up his rifle, turning halfway around as he swung to cover me.

I took a step back and shot him right through the body above the hips. I worked the lever action and shot into him again, and he fell from the saddle. His horse started forward, circled around, and stopped.

Rifle at the ready, I swept the country around, for he might not be alone. The prairie was empty, so I walked toward him. He stared up at me, hatred in his eyes. It was a wonder he was still alive.

"You wait," he said. "Andy will kill you for this."

"Maybe. . . . That's what you figured to do, didn't you? And I'm still alive."

"You goin' to let me die here?"

"Mister," I said, "You're here because you chased an old man to kill him. I'm going to see to that old man. If you're still alive when I get back to you, I'll see what I can do."

Walking over to where the wounded old man had fallen, I thought at first he was dead; but when I came up to him his eyes turned toward me. It was Harvey Bowers. He was badly shot up—how he had come any distance at all was more than I could see.

"Follered me, he done," Bowers said. "Follered me an' shot into me. The rest is dead . . . they come upon us at night . . . we figured there'd be no trouble. . . . They opened up on us." The words came slowly. "Gates was killed first off . . . Queenie done it."

"She was with them?" I asked.

"You bet—she shot Noah herself. That girl's a mean one. . . ." His voice was getting fainter.

He had taken three big ones right through the midsection. There was nothing I could do, and he wasn't asking it.

With a slight movement of his eyes he indicated Rad Miller. "Is he dead?"

"He will be. I hit him hard."

"Serves him . . . right. . . ."

It was the last thing he said, and as I straightened up I heard horses coming. It was Handy Corbin and Jim Bigbear. Jim knew both the old man and Rad, and he needed no explanation. But Corbin wanted to know about the shooting, so I told him.

"Smart," he said, "you comin' up on him like that."

"It was pure accident," I said, "and he didn't see me until I called out to him."

He gave me a wry look. "I've seen those accidents before. They only happen with a man who's careful."

We buried them on the hillside in shallow graves, and marked both graves with crosses. I said a few words over them, the murderer and the murdered, and then we rode back to our cattle, knowing trouble was coming

upon us. There was a sadness in me for old Harvey
Bowers, and for Gates as well.

They had not liked me, nor had I cared for them,
but we had shared some work together, some days and
nights of trouble; and I knew something of their problems and they knew something of mine. They were
good men, but worn by years and trouble—there are
many such. All the good men who work hard and try
to save do not end up with wealth or the good things
of this world. I imagine that Noah Gates and Harvey
Bowers had done much in their own way to open the
way west. They had pioneered where Indians roamed,
and where there was no law but what they could pro-
vide for themselves. And now they would lie in graves
soon forgotten, their trails no longer marked; their few
relatives would wait, and wait, and then gradually
would cease to wonder about them. It is not only those
who have put down foundations who have built upon
the land, for such men as Noah Gates had given of
blood and sweat and added their flesh to the soil.

We got back to the herd and moved westward. The
cattle grazed as they went along, pausing for a bite here,
a bite there. The coolness passed and the day grew
warm. Restlessly, I watched the country around.

Kelsey and Miller would begin wondering what had
become of Rad. It would be only a matter of hours
until they started hunting him, and they would surely
come upon the graves. Rad's was marked with his
name, as best we could scratch it on with a knife point.
Somebody would have been there to bury them, and
Andy Miller would want to know who it had been.

We drove into a stream and followed it up for half
a mile, with Jim or me scouting ahead to be sure there
was no quicksand. We drove out, dragged brush over
our trail for another half-mile or so, and then went
into another stream. The streams were all shallow
around here, it seemed, and neither of these had been
as much as knee-deep. When we came out of the water

we drove north. The Saline River was behind us, the South Branch not far ahead to the north.

Again we turned west, and we managed thirty miles in the next two days. By that time our horses were worn down and frazzled, and were badly needing rest.

"Any ranches west of here?" I asked Jim.

"None I know of."

He rode in silence for a few minutes and then he said, "Used to be a herd of wild stuff running between here and the Elkhorn, but mostly south of there. In the old days there were several hundred head, but last time I saw them there were only two bunches of about twenty to thirty head . . . might be others further west."

"You think we could round up a few?"

"It's worth trying," he said. "And we'll need the horses."

Tom Hacker was the best cook in the outfit, and gradually he took over the job. Each of us kept his eyes open so we could have some change in diet; sometimes it would be an antelope haunch, a few wild turkeys, or a sage hen.

It was about midafternoon when we came to a good-sized stream running about knee-deep, and we followed it northeast for a mile and a half before coming out on the bank. It was a good spot to camp, with a few cottonwoods, many willows, and some brush. The grass was good, for this was far from any trail where cattle had been driven. The route west through Nebraska lay not far to the north, but nobody traveled through the land where we rode.

Toward nightfall Handy Corbin got two sage hens. He saw them, palmed his six-gun, and fired the two shots with one sound. They were a good thirty yards off, but he nailed them both, drawing fast and smooth. I saw Hacker exchange a glance with his nephew. That was shooting, by any man's standards.

The first man into camp started a fire, and on this night it was me. Breaking some branches from a fallen limb, long dead, I gathered leaves and bark, and soon had the fire going. After I'd rustled some fuel, I returned to my horse to help get the herd bedded down.

It was a tight little camp, sheltered on one side by the thick brush and trees, and on the other by a curve of the stream where there was a high bank.

We bunched the herd tighter. The most important thing about the campsite was that it was practically invisible until a body was right on top of it. Nevertheless I was worried. We had moved far, and for much of the distance we had covered our trail, but no trail could be covered completely, and much depended on how determined they were.

Hacker gnawed at a beef bone, then tossed it into the brush, wiping his hands on the grass. "Chancy, you decided where you're goin'?" he asked. "I mean, have you picked a spot?"

"I've never been to Wyoming."

"You open for suggestions?"

"You're damned right. I'm supposed to locate these cattle on good grass and water, get some buildings up before cold weather, and get the outfit going. Now, that's a right big order, and I'm open to suggestions."

"I soldiered out here a few years back," Hacker said. "There's a big red wall cuts across the country, only one hole in it for miles, with a creek coming through. In back of that wall there's some pretty country, mighty pretty."

"We'll look at it," I told him, "though we may drive on farther. But it sounds like a place I'd like."

Long after I'd fallen asleep, I awoke and heard Cotton Madden singing "The Hunters of Kentucky." For a while I lay there, listening to his low, easy voice and watching the fire. It was then I started thinking about Kit Dunvegan, back in Tennessee.

How long before I would see her again? How would she have changed? And how would I have changed?

"That change," I said, half aloud, "will be considerable. There's room for it."

6

A cattle drive has a way of seeming to offer no change. Day after day we moved westward, the days varying only by the distance covered, the grazing we found, and the water.

We saw no human being, white man or Indian, and as we moved westward the grass became less and the soil more sandy. There were tracks of wild horses—many of them—and of antelope, which we saw almost every day, sometimes every hour of the day.

We drove our cattle, sang our songs, yarned a little around the fire at night, and came to know each other. Tom Hacker was not only the best cook, but the wisest of us all; Cotton had the best voice, and was the one most likely to be joking. Jim was by all odds the best tracker and the best rider, with Cotton a close second on the riding. Handy Corbin was considered the best shot . . . nobody questioned that—not even me.

And there was no question about who was the strongest among us, either. My work as a boy, and then on the boats and on the freight teams had given me strength, although much of it I came by naturally.

From time to time in the saddle I gave thought to myself. I felt I wasn't learning enough. Jim was teaching me about the grass, the plants, and the animals. What I hadn't known about tracking he was also teaching me, but what I needed was book-reading. I had an envy of those who could study and go to schools.

Yet in my own way I had grown a little. Being the boss had given me responsibility. I had men, horses, and cattle to consider, and the future responsibility of finding a proper ranch for Tarlton and myself.

Many a man of my age was bossing a herd or an outfit, so there was nothing unusual about that, but it does change a man when he knows others depend upon him for decisions.

Though Corbin was considered the gunfighter of the outfit, I had killed two men, but I was not anxious to have it known. I wanted no such reputation. The man I wanted to be like was Tarlton, I suppose. He was educated, respected, well dressed, and well liked. He had dignity and he was a gentleman, and these things I wanted more than anything else.

It seems to me a man comes into this world with a little ready raw material—himself. His folks can only give him a sort of push, and a mite of teaching, but in the long run what a man becomes is his own problem. There've always been hard times, there've always been wars and troubles—famine, disease, and such-like—and some folks are born with money, some with none. In the end it is up to the man what he becomes, and none of those other things matter. In horses, dogs, and men it is character that counts.

For the first time, I had a definite goal—two of them, in fact: to build a prosperous ranch, and to build myself into a man I could be pleased with. The last idea I'd had for some time, but it hadn't been formed into a goal until now. It had always been there, a sort of half-formed wish in the shadowy recesses of my mind; now it had come out into the open, and I had to do something about it.

When I went back to Tennessee I wasn't going to be just a horse thief's son. My pa had been a good man, and the best way I could convince folks they had done him wrong was by being somebody myself.

Tom Hacker rode out to where I sat my horse, watching the cattle. "You want some advice?" he said.

"Try me."

"Rest up. The horses are dead-beat. We should have twice the remuda we've got for a drive like this. If those boys catch up with us we'll make 'em wish they hadn't."

"All right. We'll do it." I hooked a leg around the pommel. "You ever read much, Tom?"

He gave me an odd look. "As a matter of fact . . . yes. When I can find something. A man can't carry much in his saddlebags." He paused. "Why do you ask?"

"This here's a big country. It's going to need big men to handle it, and I figure a big man ought to have more in his mind than I've got. Tarlton's going to send me some books, but I'm lathering to get on with it."

"I've got a couple," Hacker said. "I can't say they'd be considered an education, but they're mighty good reading." He stoked his pipe. "I've got Mayne Reid's *Afloat in the Forest*, and Richardson's *Beyond the Mississippi.*"

"I'd like to read them."

"Sure thing." He lighted his pipe. "When I left home I had four books. I swapped a *McGuffey's Reader* with a storekeeper in Missouri for a copy of *Mountains and Molehills,* by Frank Marryat. You'd never believe the number of times I've swapped books along the way. Two or three times in the army, half a dozen times out on the trail. Seems like everybody's hungry for reading, and there's mighty few books going around. I swapped that Marryat book to a gambler in Cheyenne, and three years later I was offered the very same book, with my name writ in it, in Beeville, Texas. It sure does beat all how some of these books get around."

We held the herd at that place for three days, keeping them off the horizon, and in the shallow valley along the stream. We rested ourselves and our horses, and the cattle seemed content to feed where they were. We ate, slept, yarned the hours away beside the fire; we repaired some gear, cleaned our guns, and watched the lazy cattle.

It was a good time, but in us all was the feeling that it could not last. We had been fortunate, but we were in Indian country, and somewhere out there were our enemies.

At daybreak on the third day we started them upstream, but moved them less than a mile, resting there for the last day on good fresh grass.

On the fourth day we started them again, moving them easily, letting them walk and graze, but keeping them all the time on the move toward the west. Jim, who was riding point, came back to the drag about an hour before noontime.

"I cut the trail of five shod horses," he said. "Maybe two days old . . . came in from the south. One of them was Andy Miller's."

So they were with us again. They had missed our trail, but they would pick it up somewhere ahead. Over noon coffee I drew myself a rough map in the dirt. Northwest was Cheyenne . . . further north was Fort Laramie.

"We'll try to cross the Platte somewhere near Horsetail Creek," I told the men. "If anything happens to me, Hacker will take charge and you locate on the best grass you can find and wait for word from Tarlton."

Some folks think they'll live forever, but I wasn't one of them. How long a man lasts depends on how careful he is, and on the breaks of the game. Out here in this country a bullet or an arrow was only one way to go; there were many other ways—your horse could step in a prairie-dog hole when running; you could be gored by an outlaw steer, thrown by a horse, drowned in a river-crossing, caught in quicksand, or trampled in a stampede. To say nothing of rattlers or hydrophobia skunks—those skunks sometimes bit a man on the face when he was sleeping on the prairies. It was a rough, hard land, and we learned to walk careful and keep our eyes open, trusting in the Lord and a fast gunhand.

We drove northwest while the sun blazed down and the dust clouds hung over our march, northwest across the sand dunes, over the swollen streams, up the long hills. Where water was scarce we lost some cattle, and the buzzards hung above us in the hot, empty sky. We sweated and swore and worked our horses to a frazzle, and slept when we had a chance.

And then the rains came, saving the herd and possibly ourselves, but turning the ground into a sea of mud, sometimes dimpled with the hard-striking hailstones. Tom Hacker's horse fell with him, and Tom's leg was scraped from hip to knee, his right arm badly wrenched.

Julesburg lay somewhere nearby, and we thought of it and longed for the food we could eat there that was not cooked by ourselves. We longed, too, to see other faces than those we saw every day. We drove the cattle into a hollow in the hills, rimmed by rocky cliffs. Tom, who was not able to ride with his bad leg, volunteered to stay with the herd while we rode into town. Jim offered to stay with him.

There was something inside me that warned me against Julesburg, and against leaving the herd with only two men. The town had a bad reputation, and the vicinity around was no better. But we needed supplies, and we needed the change, so Cotton, Corbin, and I rode into town.

This was the third town named Julesburg in the vicinity, and it was said by some to be the wickedest town in the country; from the beginning its history had been a bloody one.

We tied our horses at the hitching rail, but we led the pack animals around into the alley at the rear of the emporium where we expected to do our business. There we bought flour, sugar, dried fruit, coffee, and a dozen slabs of bacon, and I laid in a stock of papers and tobacco for those who smoked, and a big sack of hard candy. I also bought beans and rice, and a few cans of tomatoes. We packed it all on our pack animals, and had them ready to move out.

"Do you suppose they're in town?" Cotton asked.

"Who cares?" Corbin responded shortly. "If they come asking for it, they can have it."

"We're hunting no trouble," I said. "We'll eat, and then we'll ride out of town. Unless they come hunting us, we'll leave them alone."

Corbin stared at me. "What's the matter? You—"

"Don't say it." I was facing him. "I like you, Handy, and you're a good man, so don't say anything we'd both be sorry for. My first duty is to my partner and to those cattle, and I'm not getting myself or my men into a gun battle just to prove something to some no-accounts."

"Kelsey wouldn't like that," Corbin said with a grin. "You callin' him a no-account."

"What else is he?" was my answer to that.

The streets were crowded with rigs and wagons, and it looked as if the hitching rail was lined with saddle stock wearing every brand west of the Mississippi. We joined the crowd along the boardwalk and worked our way to the Bon Ton Restaurant, a low-roofed building with a sign hung out over the street. Inside were long, family-style tables with benches along each side.

We found places, Handy and Cotton at one table, me across the room at another. We helped ourselves and set to eating. The dishes were enameled in blue, the cups the same. It was surely better than eating whilst squatting by a fire somewhere on the trail.

Of a sudden the door opened and Caxton Kelsey came in, LaSalle Prince with him. They crossed to a table and sat down, facing Cotton and Corbin. They hadn't seen me, for I was behind them.

Kelsey hadn't seen either Cotton Madden or Corbin riding with me, and they did not seem to notice them now. But I felt sure they knew they were there. They could have seen the brands on our saddle horses, right outside. And I noticed the careful way they were studying the rest of the crowd in the Bon Ton.

Usually I am a slow eater. Today I worked my way through a stack of grub in pretty fast style, knowing there might be little time before something happened. I refilled my cup from the coffeepot, and waited.

"Noticed some saddle stock outside wearing a Lazy TC," Kelsey commented. "Who's riding for that brand?"

Before Corbin or Madden could speak, I said, "That's my brand, Kelsey. Mine and Tarlton's. Have you got some business with us?"

He turned around very slowly and looked at me. "You haven't got Hickok here to protect you today, Chancy," he said.

"Now, that's odd. I had the idea he was protecting you."

There were at least forty people in the Bon Ton, and we had all their attention by now, so I decided to create some problems for him.

"I heard some renegades hit the Noah Gates herd," I said in a voice that could be heard by everyone there, "and they killed him and murdered his partners. Then they stole the herd."

I turned to glance around the room. "Too bad . . . they were hard-up old men who drove clean up from Texas. Whoever murdered them must have been the lowest kind of coyotes."

Half a dozen voices spoke up in emphatic agreement. Then one man asked, "Do you have any idea who they were?"

"Well," I said, "the last of those old men ran to us for protection. He didn't quite make it, for he was dying when we found him, but his killer was right behind him, trying to finish him off."

"I hope you killed the skunk."

"He won't bother anybody again. His name was Rad Miller, a brother to Andy Miller, and one of the outfit he runs with."

LaSalle Prince wiped his mouth with the back of his hand. He threw his leg over the bench, keeping his back to me, and got to his feet. Fumbling in his pockets, he dug out a coin and put it on the table. All around me a buzz of conversation began, and I heard more than one man say, "They ought to be lynched!"

Caxton Kelsey was getting up, too, and I spoke again. "There's no place in the Territory for men of that stripe. I hope to see every one of them hang."

Nobody seemed inclined to argue the question, and Kelsey and LaSalle Prince were already out of the door.

Suddenly a man spoke up. "Why, I saw Andy Miller right here in town—not more'n two hours ago!"

Several men got up hurriedly, paid for their meals, and left. Handy Corbin looked over at me as I filled my cup again. "I can't quite figure you out, Chancy," he said. "You like to blew the lid off the whole thing."

I shrugged. "They won't sell any Gates cattle around here. They've got a stolen herd, but they've also got themselves a full-sized problem on what to do with it."

A big bearded man slammed down his cup and stood up. "You mean those two were among 'em?"

"The ringleaders," I said.

"Well, why the billy-be-damned didn't you say so?" he exploded. "We could have nailed 'em."

"One of those men was Caxton Kelsey," I said; "the other was LaSalle Prince. You want me to start a gun battle in here with that outfit?"

He let the air out of him and dropped back on the bench. "No, I don't—I surely don't. But you took a chance."

"I made 'em leave," I said. "Now they'll have to

move on, but I don't believe they can outrun the story that will be told."

When we rode up to the herd all was quiet, but we wasted no time. We saddled up fresh horses and moved the herd right out, driving due north.

A man ramrodding a herd of mixed stuff has got to be a worrier. He has to worry about what might happen, so he will be ready for it if it does happen; and the only thing he can be downright sure of is that if what he was afraid of doesn't happen, something else will.

Cattle are spooky, liable to scare themselves into a stampede at some sudden sound, some unexpected movement, at a flash of lightning or a rattle of pans. And every one of them seems gifted with a crazy imagination that sees ghosts, goblins, or wolves in every shadow. There may be hours on end when they plod placidly along, and then suddenly they'll be off and running . . . and a longhorn steer can cover ground like a scared antelope.

We'd been having it mighty easy so far. Our herd was trail broke, and for the greater part of the drive the grazing had been good; except for a few short drives there had been water a-plenty. But now we were entering upon a long, dusty drive over dry country, where it would be a long while between drinks.

Kelsey and his outfit knew we were driving to Wyoming, for that had been no secret, and in a town like Abilene everybody knows what everybody else is doing, anyway. My hunch was they'd cut out for Cheyenne, spend some time around the saloons and gambling houses, and then ride south to meet us sometime during the last day or so of our drive .

My guess was they'd hole up their stolen herd somewhere on a hide-out ranch run by some outlaw, and come on without it. They wanted my cattle, but most of all they wanted my hide. Now, it doesn't pay to trust too much to what you think the other fellow may do; he might do something different that would throw you off stride.

We crossed the Lodgepole and drove north across the Chugwater Flats, making easy drives to save our horses. Twice we came upon wild mustangs, but they fled on our approach; then they trailed along, always curious, always at a distance.

Jim Bigbear dropped back to where I was working the drag. No matter that I was bossing this drive—I stood my regular turn with the rest of them, and switched the bad jobs among us. The drag was the dustiest, dirtiest job of them all, and usually it was the hottest, unless the wind was stirring. Then the hottest place was on the lee side of the herd, where a body caught the heat thrown up by several hundred cattle.

"This is Cheyenne country," Jim commented, "and you'll run into the Sioux up ahead. We'd best keep an eye out for trouble."

We watered the herd, and then pushed on a couple of miles to bed them down. The best we would find was the gentle slope of a hill that offered a mite of protection from the wind.

This night I saddled the buckskin and went to scouting. First of all, I wanted to get away from the herd, for I had some thinking to do. And next, Jim had been scouting now for weeks and it was high time I did some of it, just to get better acquainted with the country, if nothing else.

When I had been scouting for nearly an hour the buckskin made his way down into a hollow among the hills. There were several cottonwoods there, and some willows . . . there might be water.

This was the route we would take tomorrow, and it would make it easy if we could water the herd well, and at the right time, so I walked the buckskin toward the trees.

The sun was low down in the sky, painting the clouds with a vivid brush. It would soon be dusk. The cottonwoods dusted their leaves together softly. There was no other sound but the soft thud of my horse's hoofs.

An Indian, rifle in hand, stood silently awaiting me. Along the edge of the wood I then saw another, and another . . . and another.

There were at least six of them, and I was alone.

7

My horse had continued to walk forward, and I lifted my right hand, palm out. Closing my fist, I then raised the index and middle fingers together, and lifted them beside my face in the sign for friend. The Indians waited, making no move.

Now, there's mighty few Indians can resist a good horse trade, and what we needed most right now was a few horses. I had a feeling these Indians could use some beef, so as I drew nearer I made the sign for trade, raising the two fore-fingers and crossing the wrists so the fingers pointed in opposite directions, and sawed the wrists back and forth a couple of times. There were some variations of these signs among plains and mountain tribes, but they mattered little.

These were Cheyennes, I could see that, and a fine-looking lot, too, warriors every one of them. They were wearing no paint, and one of them had an antelope quarter and some other meat from the animal tied in the skin behind his saddle.

One of the Indians spoke suddenly. "Who you?"

"Otis Tom Chancy. I'm driving cattle, and we could

use some horses. I figured we might swap—beef for horses."

He studied me, and then looked at the horse I was riding. Indicating the buckskin, he said, "Him Injun horse."

"I swapped for him," I said. "Got him from a Shawnee."

"What name this Shawnee?"

"Jim Bigbear. He's riding with me."

"How you know sign talk?"

"I grew up with the Cherokees." Here I made the sign for friend, then touched the fingers to my lips, which indicated brother.

Turning my horse, I motioned for them to follow, and after the briefest hesitation they trailed along behind, riding easily, but warily.

As this was Indian country we were going into, it seemed to me a good idea to try to be friends. A man can fight if he has to, but the worst thing he can do is to go looking for trouble. Of course he can make a fool of himself by assuming the other fellow wants peace, too, and this is a mistake sometimes made, for many Indians have nothing to gain except through war.

Jim saw us coming, and when we rode into camp everybody was relaxing, but at the same time everybody was armed and ready. You can be sure those Cheyennes noticed it, too.

Grub was on the fire, and Tom took one look at the Indians and started slicing chunks of beef. We sat around the fire and the Cheyennes put away the best part of a side of buffalo and a gallon or so of coffee before we settled down to palavering about horses.

Corbin sidled over to me. "You going to let them stay in camp all night?"

It was a problem, but I saw no way around it. I wanted horses, but I also wanted the Indians to know we were not afraid of them—and that if necessary we would fight.

By the time darkness was closing in we had made us

a swap of beef for horses. They would ride back to their camp for the horses, and then we would make the swap. But we wanted *good* horses . . . this was the point I made. Good stock, or no trade.

As a matter of fact, I needed those horses almighty bad. Ours were worn down from overwork, and we were nearing the country where I planned to settle. Once there, we would have to keep a constant watch on our herds or Indians would run them off, and at the same time we would have to be building corrals, a cabin for ourselves, and some kind of shelter for our saddle stock.

Jim Bigbear was taking the first guard, and when he rode out the Cheyennes watched him go. These Indians looked fit for any kind of a scrap. We were five to their six, but aside from our six-shooters we were no better armed.

Tom and Cotton turned in, and the Indians rolled up in their blankets, but none of us was fooled. We knew they would be awake, or at least some of them would. After a while, Handy Corbin went to his blankets, and I sat alone by the fire, rifle across my knees.

It was quiet . . . we heard nothing but a coyote howling in the far-off distance. The cattle bedded down and seemed content. After a time I went to my blankets and turned in, but I kept a six-gun in my hand, and my rifle close by.

Cotton got up shortly before midnight, added some water to the coffee, and Tom joined him. Cotton rode out to relieve Jim, and after having his coffee, Tom went out, too. Jim idled about the fire and I went to sleep with him still there. We had agreed amongst us that either Tom or Cotton would ride up to the fire off and on during the night to sort of keep an eye on things after Jim turned in.

It was about two hours after midnight that I woke up. It was time for Handy and me to relieve the others. For a few minutes I lay still, just listening, studying the night with my ears.

From where I lay I could see the fire, which was down to red coals. There was some smoke drifting up, mingling with a mite of steam from the pot. All of a sudden I saw one of the Indians move under his blanket. He came out from under it like a snake, and he had a knife in his hand.

I don't know what he had in mind. With an Indian, a body never knows. We had a lot of fixings around camp that an Indian could use, and to an Indian anybody not of his tribe is fair game. To his way of thinking, to stick a knife into each one of us would be a fine piece of business. But I wanted no trouble unless it was necessary, so I merely eared back the hammer of my Winchester.

That Cheyenne froze as if somebody had nailed his feet to the ground, but I just got up, easy-like and walked over to the fire, seeming to pay him no mind. He could see the hammer was back on my Winchester, and he could make his own choices.

He simply picked up a stick and began cutting some shavings to kindle up the fire, as if that had been his idea all the time . . . and maybe it was.

The fire began to blaze up and I poured him a cup of coffee and handed it across the fire to him—with my left hand. And he taken it, also with his left hand. I thought I glimpsed a bit of a twinkle in his eyes.

We both drank coffee, and then Corbin came up to the fire. I could tell from his eyes that he, too, had been awake. And so could the Cheyenne. If he had lifted that knife to anybody, he would have been blasted right out of his tracks by at least two rifles . . . and well he knew it.

When daylight came the Indians rode off, and a few hours later they were back with some saddle stock. We made a swap, picking up six fresh ponies, and the Cheyennes left with us a buffalo quarter for good measure.

We shook hands, that big Cheyenne and me, and

grinned at each other. Neither of us was fooled, and each of us was liking the other.

He had walked his horse some thirty yards when he turned in the saddle. "Where you go?"

"Somewhere up on the Powder."

"That's Cheyenne country."

"We don't figure to cause any trouble. We're just going to run a few head of cattle up there. You come and see me. I'll have a beef for you."

They rode away, and we watched them go, and then we started our cattle again.

In the cool of the evening we came up to the red wall that Tom Hacker had told me about. We'd been taking our time, and the cattle were fat and sassy. The wall towered up above the grassy plain, barring all progress.

"You say there's a hole in that? How far up?"

"I'm guessing," Jim said, after studying the country and the wall, "but I'd say four, five miles north. The Middle Fork of the Powder runs through it, and it's a big, wide hole. That's not to say that a few riflemen couldn't hold it if they were of a mind to. There's water and grass in behind it . . . good grazing along Buffalo or Spring creeks."

A couple of hours later we rode through the Hole-in-the-Wall and let the herd spread out a mite along the Middle Fork. It was almost dark, but we let them eat a little before we bunched them for the night.

Two days later we found the spot we were searching for, a hollow of the hills with some scattered trees and brush, and a creek that turned around under the edge of the fringing cliffs that shaded the water. It was good water, sweet and cold. There was good grass around, mostly blue grama on the flatlands and low hills, wheatgrass on the higher ridges.

We turned the herd loose in the rock-walled basin and set to work to build a cabin under the trees. Hacker, Madden, and I did most of the building, while

Handy Corbin and Jim Bigbear guarded the cattle.
They sometimes killed an antelope or a deer, and once
in a while a buffalo. The weeks passed quickly, and
there was no sign of trouble.

"You think we lost 'em?" Madden asked me.

"No," I said, "they'll be coming."

"I feel that you are right," Jim Bigbear commented
soberly.

As the best hand with an axe, I notched the logs for
the cabin. We could expect cold winters, and we made
the cabin tight and strong, allowing no chinks, and we
built a good fireplace that would take a good-size log.
But every day, no matter how heavy the work load, I
managed to let one rider loose to explore the country.
At night we'd talk about what he'd seen during the day,
and as most cowhands have a good feeling for terrain
and the general lay of the land, we soon began to get a
picture of what it was like around our ranch.

"We're going to have to cut hay," I told them, "so
keep an eye out for some good meadows."

We snaked logs out of the timber, taking the fallen
stuff wherever possible, and building a stack of wood
against the coming winter. And in all that time we saw
nobody at all, not even an Indian.

By the time the cool winds started to blow down off
the mountains we had wood stacked near the cabin, hay
stacked in the meadows, and near one of the cliffs that
bordered our little basin we had built a shelter for cattle
that used the wall of the cliff to keep the wind off them.
We had worked hard and steady, and still no trouble.

But I was worried. Not so much by what might happen when Caxton Kelsey and LaSalle Prince found us
as by thinking of Tarlton's coming.

When we made our deal in Abilene he had said he
would join us with another herd this year. That meant
he'd best be getting here soon if he was coming. There
was no post office within many a mile, and it seemed as
if the best chance to get some news was to ride to
Cheyenne, or to Fort Laramie, which was a bit closer.

Also, if he had a herd on the trail we'd best be keeping an eye out for it. All Tarlton knew was that we had come to Wyoming.

Now, that wasn't so bad as it might sound, because cattle were so scarce in Wyoming in 1871 that word of mouth would tell him a good bit about where we'd gone. But he would never find this place without a guide.

The upshot of it was that I started thinking of riding down the trail toward Fort Laramie. The work here was caught up. Now it was mostly a matter of keeping a watch on the cattle and riding careful because of Indians, so I put it up to them. "I'm fixing to take two men along," I said, "and you can draw cards for who's to go."

Corbin and Hacker won, but Hacker tossed his winning king back on the deck. "Take Cotton along," he said. "He's younger, and he'll need a look at a girl before he holes in for the winter."

The leaves had turned, the grass had gone all brown, and the winds that blew down from the Big Horns were raw and cold. When a man starts riding out in that kind of weather it makes him wonder what he's done with his summer's wages.

We went out of the Hole-in-the-Wall and lit a shuck for Fort Laramie. We had been riding no more than an hour when we crossed the first set of tracks—a dozen ponies, unshod, heading west, and a bit south.

"No travois," Corbin said, "so they're not just moving to another camp. No women or kids along."

"Might be a hunting party," Cotton Madden suggested.

We rode on, but just before sundown we came on another bunch of tracks, also headed a little south of west . . . only four riders this time.

Nobody was taking any bets, but we were all doing some serious contemplating. So far, it didn't mean a thing, but there'd been talk here and there of the Chey-

ennes getting together, with rumors of them going on
the warpath.

Fort Laramie was the biggest army post I'd seen. It
lay on the flat in a bend of the Laramie River, named
for a French-Canadian trapper, Jacques La Ramée, who
was killed by Indians in 1820. The fort had first been a
fur-trading post, back in 1834, and folks bound west
had stopped off there for many a year.

It was quite a place, with a lot of buildings of all sorts
scattered about, maybe half of them around the parade
ground, the rest seemingly located without any plan.
The hills around were brown with autumn, and most of
the trees along the river had already shed their leaves.

We rode up to the sutler's store, dismounted, tied our
horses, and went inside. There were three men at the
enlisted men's bar . . . only one of them a soldier.

The bartender moved over to us, polishing a glass.
"Rye," I said, "and some information."

He filled our glasses, then squinted through the cigarette smoke, resting both hands on the bar. "What do
you want to know?" he asked.

"We're expecting a herd of cattle . . . a small herd.
A man named Tarlton will probably bring them."

"Cattle? We haven't seen a herd of cattle, not since
I've been on the post. Only cattle I've seen was driven
in here for our own use."

One of the men at the bar, a stocky man in buckskins, turned half around. "Tarlton? The cattle buyer
from Abilene? He rode out of Abilene before I did . . .
that's a month ago."

Corbin tossed off his drink. "We've got troubles,
Chancy," he said. "He should have been here before
this."

"Any Indian trouble?" I asked.

"None to speak of," the man in buckskins answered.
"Of course, you know how it is with Indians, if they get
notional. Where were the cattle headed?"

Well, I hesitated. I knew the army looked with no

favor on cattlemen moving into Indian country. "Up the country," I said finally.

"You'd better have your own army then. The Sioux don't take to the white-eyes moving in amongst them."

"I thought that was Cheyenne country."

"Sioux . . . Cheyenne, it makes no difference, They'll have your hair if you try to live in that country." He paused. "A man might make peace with the Cheyennes, although they are great fighters when given cause. But I don't believe the devil himself, nor the good Lord, for that matter, could make peace with the Sioux. They live to fight, and believe me, friend, they fight well."

Of their fighting ability I had no doubt, but I hoped to live among them in peace. The buffalo were going, anybody could see that, and maybe we could trade with the Indians . . . maybe even get them to ranching on shares.

What worried me right now was Tarlton. He should have arrived near Fort Laramie by now, or he should have gone on north, and we had cut no trail coming south.

We went outside. It was pleasantly warm in the sunshine, cool in the shade. I glanced at the sky, and it gave promise of fair weather. But I had no idea what to do. Seems to me a lot of folks want to be leaders, but almighty few of them realize that decisions don't come easy. We could wait here, hoping Tarlton would show up, or we could scout toward Nebraska, or even send out a man to ride west and try to cut any trail they might have made.

Finally I decided to sit tight and keep my boys together. Meanwhile I would try to find out if any patrols or army details had been sent out, and to learn what they knew. That meant caution, for if the army had to notice us officially, we'd be in the soup for sure.

I couldn't stop thinking of Tarlton. He was a good man, but he was a city man. I had no idea who he had with him, or how good they were, and I knew a good part of my own success had been because of the men

I'd had with me. Especially because of the uncanny skill of Jim Bigbear and the steadiness of Tom Hacker. But every man had done his share.

Also, the more I heard of the Sioux and the Cheyennes, the more worried I became for the herd and the men left with it. I not only wanted to find Tarlton, but I wanted to be back with the outfit. The Indians would surely know where they were, and might come down upon them at any time.

We went back into the sutler's store and bought what we could, letting him hold it for us until we decided to leave. To the other things, we added ammunition. I had no idea how much we'd need, but I bought a thousand rounds.

The sutler stared. "You figuring on starting a war?"

"Buffalo huntin'," I lied. "I heard there was a big lot of them over west and to the south."

Probably he didn't believe me, but he let us have what we wanted.

We stayed at the post for two full days, checking every rumor we heard, talking to the soldiers who returned from the routine patrols. But all the while we heard nothing.

When the news came it was bad . . . very bad.

I was sitting with Corbin at a table in the sutler's saloon when Cotton came in. He crossed right over to the table and pulled back a chair. "Chancy"—he spoke in a low tone, but I could see the others watching, guessing something was in the wind—"I seen a cowhide hangin' on a fence yonder." He jerked his head to indicate the direction of Hog Town. "It's carryin' a Lazy TC!"

"You sure?" I asked it, but I was only buying time to consider, for I knew he was sure. No cowhand was apt to mistake something like that.

"I'm sure," he said. "I'd have started askin' folks about it, but decided I'd best get back here and report to you."

"Good man," I said. "Let's go over there."

We got up and went outside to our horses. As we mounted up, I glanced over by the commissary. There was a man standing there watching us, and there was something vaguely familiar about him, but I gave it no special thought at the moment.

The Hog Ranch was a saloon, trading post, and hotel just off the post at the western end. Later it would become a more elaborate setup, I suppose, but right then it was a pretty miserable place, offering the soldiers some rot-gut whiskey, a change of food, and occasionally, a woman or two imported from bigger towns where they hadn't been able to stand the competition. Officially, it didn't even exist, but every man on the post knew it was there, and knew it as a hangout for some rough types.

We rode up and dismounted in front of the saloon. Cotton glanced toward the fence, and whispered to us. "They've taken it in. The hide's gone."

We walked into the saloon, and a much less knowing man than any of us could have seen that they had staked us out and all but nailed our hides to the wall.

The bartender was a big man, inclined toward jowls and belly, with sleeves rolled up and a dirty apron on. At the end of the bar a sour-faced man with a tied-down gun was standing. Two other men sat at a table, and one of them had his hand under the flap of his coat. Two more men came in the door behind us as we stepped in and looked around.

"There was a hide on the fence out there," I said. "I want to know where it came from."

Nobody said anything at all. They just looked at us, waiting.

"Somebody might have found a stray," I said, "and I am going to take it that way if you tell me where you got it."

The gunman at the end of the bar said carelessly, "We don't care how you take it, kid."

Handy Corbin had turned so he was facing the table, and Cotton Madden was looking at the two men who

had come in behind us, but I wasn't thinking about
them. I was close up to the bar by then, and I back-
handed the gunman across the mouth.

He wasn't expecting anything like that. They thought
they had us boxed, and that we'd back out or get gunned
down. He was hardly through speaking when I struck,
and I struck almighty fast. Like I've said, I'm figured to
be an uncommonly strong man—my hands are hard,
and there's considerable muscle behind them.

It was a wicked blow, and he staggered back, trip-
ping over a chair so that he fell against the wall, his
lips split and dripping blood. Dazed, he put a hand to
his mouth, and when he saw the blood he started to go
for his gun.

What triggered my hands, I'll never know, but an
instant before he moved my rifle swung up and I shot
into him just as his hand grasped his gun butt.

He turned a mite, drawing, and I reckon it saved his
life for hanging, for my bullet struck his hip right above
the holster, knocking him sideways. The bullet hit the
hipbone, then glanced off and sheered a small chunk
from the meaty part at the base of his gunhand.

My rifle was right on him and I'd worked the lever of
the Winchester without even thinking of it. The muzzle
was on his belly, and I wasn't six feet away. He was
shocked by the smash of the bullet, and he was scared.
He was looking right into the hollow eye of death, and
he knew it.

"Now just you wait," he said, thickly, "you hold up
there, mister. You ain't hunting me."

What was taking place behind me, I didn't know,
but that was up to Corbin and Madden, and I knew
them both. They'd stand their ground. The truth was
the suddenness of my shot kind of stunned those others.
They'd reckoned this was their party, and the change
in the state of things was too fast for them.

"I want to know where that hide came from," I said,
"and you'd better start talking."

Out of the corner of my eye I saw the bartender's

hand drop off the bar and I swung my rifle barrel in a
short, vicious chop that caught him on the side of the
head. He dropped as if he'd been shot, and I brought
my gun muzzle back on the gunman's belly. "You're
talking, mister," I said, "and you'd better make it clear
the first time. I'm in no good mood."

"I had no hand in it," he said, gripping his wounded
hand, which was oozing great drops of blood. "They
drove some beef in here and peddled it for drinkin'
money."

"Who was it? And when?"

"It was Satiday. There was three of them. Three men
and a woman . . . a redheaded woman."

"How many head?"

"Ten, twelve head, maybe."

I looked at the bartender. "You bought them?"

While I was talking Corbin had stepped around the
bar and taken up the shotgun the bartender kept there.
He had picked the bartender up and was holding him
with one hand. The big man had a nasty cut along his
skull above his ear and a stunned glaze to his eyes. I
had to ask the question again before he could answer.

"Uh-huh. I bought 'em."

"You bought stolen stock," I said, "and the going
price in Abilene was twenty dollars a head. We'll figure
there was ten head, and that means you owe me two
hundred dollars."

He stared at me, trying to face me down. "I bought
that stock," he muttered. "I paid for 'em!"

"They were stolen cattle, and you knew it," I said,
"and they were my cattle. If you say they were not
stolen, and that you didn't know it, you're a liar on
both counts. Pay me."

He hesitated, but Corbin shook him so his teeth
rattled, and he fumbled in his pocket and counted out
ten gold eagles on the bar.

"Write him out a bill of sale; Cotton," I said, "and
I'll sign it."

Corbin had shoved the bartender against the bar, and

he was holding the shotgun on the other men. I waved the gunman around and he staggered over and fell into a chair at the table.

"You goin' to let me do something about this hand?" he pleaded.

"Just as much as you'd have done for me." I said. "If you're alive when we leave here, you can do something about it then. Right now I want to know where those men went . . . the ones who sold the cattle. And don't waste any more time by saying you don't know."

One of the men at the table wet his lips. "Hell, it ain't no sweat off us. They rode in from the south, and they went back that way. They were askin' about another herd of Lazy TC cattle. We hadn't seen 'em. He was also askin' about you . . . if you're Chancy."

"I'm Chancy," I said, "Otis Tom Chancy. And if you see those boys again, you tell 'em I'm looking for them. And if they've killed my partner, Bob Tarlton, I'll see they hang."

We started toward the door. "And that goes for anybody who lends them a hand, or buys any more cattle from them."

Outside the air was cool. We swung into our saddles, Handy Corbin still carrying the shotgun.

He glanced over at me as we started to ride away. "Mister," he said, "you can sure build yourself a fire if you've got the right kindling."

8

At the sutler's store we split our supplies, taking what we could pack on one horse. We left the other supplies with him, and turned the rest of our stock into his corral. Briefly, I explained what had happened, and left word with him for Tarlton if he should happen to come in before we did . . . if he was still alive.

We followed a south-bound trail. There was no use hunting for tracks until well away from the fort. Army patrols and folks coming and going would have trampled all sign into a mess of tracks imposed upon tracks.

Five miles south, when the tracks had thinned out, I described the tracks of Andy Miller's horse and that big black of Kelsey's to Cotton Madden and Handy Corbin. "We'll camp tonight," I said, "and in the morning Corbin will ride east and Cotton west. Five miles should do it. If either of you boys comes on the Kelsey lot, don't start a war all by yourselves—cut the rest of us in on it."

"You figure there's been shootin'?" Cotton asked.

"I don't know. Only Kelsey's outfit seems to have a pattern of holding the main herd back in the hills, and driving a few head into town to sell. Like as not we'll find the herd somewhere south of here."

At daybreak, after a quick cup of coffee, we started out. When the others had gone, I taken my rifle from the scabbard and started south, leading the pack horse and studying the ground in long sweeps to right and left.

Now, most Indians travel by landmarks, and if a body can figure which landmarks an Indian is using, he can afford to pay little attention to tracks on the ground. But these were white men, not as canny at hiding a trail as an Indian is, yet smart enough not to be taken lightly.

I moved slowly south. The sun climbed into the sky, the day grew warm. I found occasional buffalo tracks, and several small herds of antelope started up and ran off, but I saw no tracks of riders. I studied the terrain with care, for I was wary of ambush.

Suddenly in the eastern sky there rose a trail of smoke. Dismounting, I hurriedly put together a few clumps of sage and lighted them to signal Cotton Madden, in case he had not seen the original smoke.

Corbin hadn't waited. Cotton rode up shortly after I came up to where he had been, and we found the remains of the fire and an arrow of stones indicating the trail, which was a good fifty feet from the fire.

Corbin's own trail was alongside the trail of the four riders and two pack horses. We started on at a trot, for that trail was a good three to four days old. Evidently they were not worried about being followed, for their tracks led straight away, and surely they had not reason to suspect we were anywhere around, nor anybody else who might be interested in following them.

They had made their nooning under some cottonwoods beside a small stream, and from the looks of things they had taken their time. The tracks indicated that they had loafed about, perhaps napped a short time, and drank some beer. The bottles were close by.

When Kelsey and the others had started on again, their pace was leisurely.

Handy Corbin, on the other hand, was pushing hard. So we were left with no choice—we had to ride fast ourselves, or let Corbin come upon them alone.

Suddenly the trail turned at right angles and dipped into a draw. At this point, Corbin had swung wide, not liking the change, and he had ridden on ahead, scouting the draw from some distance away. Then he had dismounted, left his horse among some brush, and had crawled up to the arroyo.

There was nothing about it that I liked. Corbin was moving too fast . . . he should have waited for us. Drawing rein, I sat my saddle and listened, and for a while I heard no sound but the slight creak as Madden eased his weight in the saddle, or the shifting of a hoof by one of the horses.

My eyes scanned the country ahead, taking in every clump of brush or rocks, every dip or hollow that I could see. Without any reason I could name, I was feeling uneasy. I felt a soft breeze stir along my cheek, but there was no other motion. There seemed to be nothing around us but the desert.

Touching a heel to my horse, I started him forward at a walk. The logical thing was to slip up to the edge of that arroyo and look over . . . or ride up and look over. A body would just naturally want to see what Handy Corbin had seen . . . if anything.

"Cotton"—I spoke low, without even turning my head—"you take the lead rope on this pack horse. When I give the word you break hard to your right and ride like hell. There's a hollow yonder. You get into it and ride for the draw up ahead. I'm going in right here."

If they were waiting for us—and I had my hunch they were—they'd be thrown off balance when we split in opposite directions.

Softly, I spoke to my horse. "All right, boy," I said, "here we go!"

I felt his muscles tense, and when I said, *"Now!"* I
let him have the spurs. He jumped as if he'd been shot,
and we lit out on a scramble for the arroyo. Into it we
went, rifle in my hand, and swiftly wheeling him I
charged up the arroyo.

There was a muffled shot, then I rounded the bend
in the arroyo and they were there, dead ahead of me.
Pointing the rifle with one hand, like a pistol, I shot
into the nearest man at point-blank range.

They had expected us to ride together, and they had
expected us to try to get away. Instead, we had split
apart evidently just as one of them shot.

My horse was at a dead run when I came on them,
and when my shot went off my rifle muzzle wasn't
more than six feet from the man's chest. The bullet
slammed him down, and a hoof from my horse caught
him as he fell.

The other man, the one who had fired, was caught
without warning. He was up at the edge of the arroyo,
and his footing there was bad. As he turned sharply
around to bring his gun to bear, the sand gave way
beneath him and he slid, off balance, to the bottom of
the arroyo.

Still holding my rifle like a pistol, I tried a shot at
him and missed by three feet, my horse still charging
forward. I spun him around—and like any good cutting
horse, he could turn on a dime and have five cents left
—and he turned, just barely making it in the narrow
confines of the arroyo.

The fallen man was scrambling to his feet, a stocky
man with red hair whom I had never seen before. His
face was red, his pale blue eyes were staring wild, and
his lips were drawn back. He had dropped his rifle and
was coming up with a six-gun. There was no time . . .
I charged my horse into him and knocked him spinning
into the rocks, and his gun flew from his hand.

My horse stopped and swung around and I held my
rifle on the sprawled-out man, for an instant hesitating

whether to shoot or not. He saw it and threw out a hand. "For God's sake, man! Don't shoot!"

"You came hunting me," I said, still holding the rifle on him.

Desperately, I wanted to look at the first man. Was he dead, or only injured? I side-stepped my horse until I could see them both. The other man was lying still, no weapon within sight.

Were there more of them? "If you want to live, mister," I said, "you'd better start talking, and if I even take a notion that you are lying, I'll put one into your brisket and leave you here."

"Don't shoot!" he pleaded again. "Look, I'm all busted up as it is. I don't know how bad."

"Pretty bad," I said. "Who put you up to this?"

I could see their horses now, and I knew one of them. It was one of the Gates horses, stolen when the cattle were stolen, no doubt.

"That Queenie woman. She said it would be easy, an' she offered us thirty dollars apiece for you all."

"Where is she now?"

"Yonder, I expect, over at the Forks with the herd."

"How'd she know we'd be coming?"

"Damned if I know. Cax, he didn't think you were anywhere around, but that redhead . . . she knew. She swore you'd be coming; but if you didn't, we were to ride on up to Fort Laramie and nose around until you did come."

"What happened to Corbin?"

"Who's he?"

"Handy Corbin . . . he was ahead of us."

"*Handy* Corbin? The hell you say! We saw nothing of him, mister . . . and if we had he'd have only seen us runnin'. I want no piece of him—he's Hell on wheels!"

"So you got me instead. All right, you keep talking. Are there any more of you out here?"

"No."

"How many at the Forks?"

He hesitated. He was growing more wary, so I told him where he stood. "Listen, you talk, or I'll take your horse and leave you. I don't know how bad you're busted and I don't care, but my guess is you've got yourself a few busted bones. You know about how long you'd last out here without a horse, without water, without a gun."

He wet his lips. His face was becoming pale now, and I had a hunch he was beginning to feel the pain as the shock wore off. He might be only bruised, but a badly bruised bone can trouble a man as much as a broken one.

"There's nine, all told," he said. "That's including the women. There's the redhead and there's Steve Camden's woman. Seven men."

"What's there? I mean, what's at the Forks? Is it a hide-out for thieves, or a ranch or what?"

"It's Camden's ranch . . . the Circle C. Two of the boys there work for him. The others just holed up there for one reason or another."

Urged by my gun muzzle and a few threats, he kept on talking, once he'd got started. Camden's place was an outlaw hide-out, with fresh horses and meals always available . . . at a price. Also, stolen cattle could be pastured there.

There had been an attack on a herd by Caxton Kelsey's outfit, and they had lost a man, with two others wounded. They had killed at least two men, and had driven the others wounded and afoot, into the sand hills. The survivors, if there were any left by now, were without water, without horses.

Persistent urging from me brought out the fact that Kelsey kept a man on a butte with field glasses, watching for anybody coming north. If any survivors did manage to get that far they would be hunted down and killed. There was, the wounded man assured me, no chance at all for anybody to get by that butte unseen, either going or coming.

Cotton Madden came riding back down the arroyo

leading the pack horse. He had seen nobody. So where was Corbin?

We went over to the other man. He was still unconscious, but he was breathing. When I had come charging in, holding the rifle in one hand, my bullet, which I had tried to aim low, had actually glanced off his skull. The scalp was ripped open, and he probably had a concussion.

Cotten found a few sticks of wood in the bottom of the arroyo and we put together a small fire. After collecting their guns, I helped the red-headed man up. One leg was badly wrenched, although it did not seem to be broken, and the back of his shirt was soaked with blood from deep lacerations caused by falling on the sharp-edged rocks. His arm was scraped, and there was something wrong with the elbow—it looked as if it might be broken. I might have tried setting a leg or an arm, but an elbow was something I didn't want to tackle.

"We're going to make some coffee," I said, "and you're welcome. Then you better mount up and head for Fort Laramie and the sawbones at the fort. You've got a bad arm there . . . I think something is busted."

"You turning us loose?" the redhead asked.

"We don't want any part of you," I said. "We could shoot you, but you'd likely poison all the buzzards in the country. So we're turning you loose . . . only we'll keep your guns."

"Now, wait a minute!" he protested. "You leave us with no guns, and the first Indian we meet will have our scalps."

I grinned at him. "Red, you better heist your heels for the fort. If you can pray, and if you're lucky, you won't meet any Indians."

He grumbled some, but I was of no mind to give the guns back to men who had shot at me. "What about him?" he said, and gestured toward the still unconscious outlaw.

"You carry him along," I said. "I figure he'll come to before long. There's one more thing, though. I'd take it most unkind if I found you on my trail again. If I was you I'd get fixed up at the fort, and then when you're able to travel you head for the Nation, or anywhere I'm not likely to be."

We gave them coffee and turned them loose, and then tied the spare rifles on our pack horse, and stuck the spare pistols in our bags. That made two extras I had, for I was still packing the gun I'd taken off the would-be sheriff.

There was still no sign of Handy Corbin. We studied around, hoping to pick up his trail, but he'd left no more tracks than a ghost.

The country before us looked open, but actually it was not. Long ago I had discovered that much of the western plains or desert terrain can fool a man, for where it looks flat or only gently rolling there may be deep hollows or draws that cannot be seen until a man is right up to them.

We came suddenly on the trail of the cattle when we were thinking only of the trail of Caxton Kelsey and his partners. Cotton was off to one side, maybe a quarter of a mile east of me at the moment, and he was the first to see the tracks.

He rode over to join me, following the tracks down to where they intersected our own trail. At this stage the herd was walking, and superimposed on the tracks of the cattle were those of the riders who rode the drag. One of them was Kelsey's black.

"Where do we go from here?" Cotton asked. He squinted his eyes into the distance toward where the cattle had gone. The trail was several days old, and was already beginning to dust over, but we could pick it up easy enough. What was bothering me was Tarlton and those riders he had with him—riders that were working for me as well as for him.

"We'll go back," I said. "Maybe all of those boys are dead, but we'll give them a decent burial, and if there are any still alive we'll find them."

"It's been a while," Cotton said.

"Those were tough men," I said, "and a tough man with a will to live is a hard man to kill. If Tarlton wasn't shot dead, he's making a fight for it somewhere right this minute. We'll ride back."

"What about Handy?"

"He'll have to go his own way. He took off on some wildgoose chase or other, so he's on his own. He might have gone off there," I gestured toward the east, where the herd had come from, "and he might have followed the herd."

"He's a hunting man," Madden said. "He'd follow the herd."

"Luck to him," I said. "We'll ride east."

We turned our horses and rode along the dusty trail. My eyes searched the sky. I knew what I was looking for, and Cotton knew enough not to need to ask.

I was watching for buzzards.

9

Above the sagebrush levels where no cattle grazed, the buzzards hung almost motionless against the sky. We had seen them from well over a mile back, and rode warily, with fear for what we might find. We rode in silence—there was only the creak of our saddles, only the hoof-falls of our horses.

The first thing we came on was a horse. It lay sprawled in death, the saddle gone. Beyond was the body of a man, a stranger. He had been stripped of clothing and mutilated.

"No Injun did that," Cotton said. "It was somebody trying to make it look like Injun work."

We spread out, to cover more ground. We found another body; this time the mutilation had been hasty, as somebody might do who was in a hurry and wanted to get it over with; it was not done with the thoroughness of an Indian who did not want to meet an armed and dangerous enemy in the happy hunting grounds.

Cotton lifted his arm and I rode over to him. In a buffalo wallow there was another dead horse—it had been a mighty fine animal—and the earth was torn up by much moving around. A body could see where boot toes had been dug into the ground by a man who lay on his belly shooting. And he *had* been shooting. Cotton counted forty-two cartridge cases. Somebody had made quite a stand here.

Superimposed on the tracks were the tracks of a shod horse, or horses. One of the cartridge shells had been tramped into the ground.

"Whoever it was, he got away," I said to Madden.

"For a while, anyway. Must've been he stood them off until dark, then slipped off. These horseshoe tracks must've been made when they came hunting him and found him gone."

We circled, studying the sign. Clouds were gathering . . . wind whipped our hatbrims, stirred the dust. "Goin' to rain," Madden remarked. "I wonder what became of Corbin." But we had no answer to that.

We found a trail, quite by accident, it seemed. We had started to turn away to check toward the east when I saw a smudge underneath the edge of a clump of sage. "Look here," I said.

"Well, I'll be damned," Cotton Madden said, and he studied the track, then looked up. "Smart . . . he took off his boots. He's in his sock feet."

The prints were vague, indefinite, but we knew what to look for now, and we found it. There was another, more defined print a bit farther on. He was beginning to hurry . . . but they had not looked this far, and they had been looking for boot tracks.

For an hour we worked steadily at the trail, sometimes losing it, then finding it again, hoping to find the man, who might be wounded. It was a case of by guess and by God.

He had traveled half a mile before he stopped to put on his boots. We found that track by obvious means. When we ran out of sign we sat our saddles and contemplated the situation. Where would a man go who desperately needed to hide?

We scanned the country. On a ridge nearby there were rocks and trees, and off to the west was rough low ground with scattered brush.

"I'll gamble on the low ground," I said. "This hombre is smart, whoever he is. He'd figure on them looking up yonder."

"I think you're right," Madden said, "but I'll ride up there anyway."

In the low ground I found the place where he had stopped to pull on his boots, and he had walked on from there. By that time his feet must have been sore.

The low ground turned out to be some old wallows, with a cut where run-off water had headed for the creek. He had followed that slight cut, scarcely deep enough to cover a creeping man, down to the creek bed.

That creek wasn't much. Dry now, in wet weather it must have run with a good stream. There were traces in the bottom of recent water . . . it had probably been there only a short time before our man came along. He might even have found a drink.

We scouted both ways, and found his trail going upstream. He had stopped often to rest. "Must be wounded," Cotton said.

"Or maybe he's a city man, not used to rough walking."

"You think it's Tarlton?"

"Could be," I said.

A few spattering drops of rain fell, and we went into our blanket rolls for our slickers and put them on. The rain fell harder, and cut visibility. It was a cold rain, driven by a stiff wind that kept our hatbrims slapping our brows.

"This'll wipe out the tracks," Cotton said.

"He'll stay with the stream bed. It's his best chance to find water . . . a pool somewhere, or maybe a spring."

We did find an occasional track, but the rain was already making them shapeless. Despite the fact that the man was tired and perhaps wounded, he kept going. "He's got sand," Cotton said. "I'll give him that."

The rain became a downpour. Our horses splashed through gathering pools, and a trickle started in the stream bed. We searched the banks for any hide-out, even the simplest shelter, or for anyplace where he might have climbed out of the stream. Occasionally we ourselves rode our horses up the bank and studied the country. It was gently rolling, with here and there a bluff or a somewhat steeper hill, barren of any but the simplest growth.

Ahead of us was a bank where the stream at high water had cut away the rocky edge. Somebody had rolled down slabs of rock and set up a few drift logs to make a crude shelter.

"How about some coffee?" Cotton suggested.

Our horses needed the rest more than we did, and there was room enough for them under the overhang.

"It's a wonder he didn't stop here," Cotton said. "I'll make coffee if you want to look around."

We got down from our saddles and led the horses under the overhang. There was plenty of fuel, and Cotton built a fire. Knocking the water from my hat, I looked around me.

This was an obvious spot for our man to find shelter —that might be why he had not stopped . . . if he had not. He might have thought they knew of this place.

"There's been a fire," Cotton said. "Look at that charcoal. The edges are still sharp. Charcoal wears down mighty fast in wind and rain."

"No rain in here . . . but you're right, Cotton. Still, we can't bank on anything."

With the rain pounding down. I prowled about. Soon I could smell the coffee, and then the bacon. I turned to start back—it was a casual glance over my shoulder that stopped me.

There was a place where a great old tree on the bank leaned far over, branches dropping down to make a sort of natural stable. The falling rain, the darkness of the rain clouds, and the shadow of the tree, all so ob-

scured my view that I had to look again to be sure of
what I saw. A horse was there, standing three-legged,
head drooping.

The place was somewhat beyond the shelter where
Cotton Madden was making coffee. It was just around
a slight bend in the creek, and in a sort of notch just a
few feet out of line with the stream bed, and the eyes
just naturally carried on beyond, upstream.

Rifle ready, I walked slowly forward, studying the
rocks around, the tree itself, for any possible point of
concealment. But there was nothing of the sort.

As I came close I recognized the horse—it was another of Gate's horses. And then I saw the body.

A man in a checkered shirt lay on his face near the
horse's head. One hand gripped a half-drawn pistol. He
had been shot at close range, and in the act of drawing;
and he had been shot right through the skull.

There had been another horse here, and another
man. Had that man killed this one? Or had there been
another, unseen attacker?

I stood there for a moment, looking down at the dead
man, and could not help but wonder how he had come
to this. It is a question that often comes when one looks
upon death, I suppose, as if one might find some com-
mon denominator. He was an ordinary-looking man,
who under other conditions might have found steady
employment somewhere, making a modest bit of money.
No telling what this man might have been, or had been.

Who had killed him? Had it been Tarlton? Or one
of our other men? After all, I knew none of them, for
Tarlton would have hired them after I had started west.
Only it was a cinch that any man riding a Gates horse
was an outlaw, for the horses had been stolen.

One thing was certain: two men must have stopped
here. One had killed the other and ridden off; or somebody else had killed this man, taken the other horse and
departed, leaving this horse for the other man. Which
would mean that other man was somewhere about. But

the horse had been tied more than one day, which posed another question.

Taking the bridle, I led him to the stream for a drink. He drank long and thirstily, and as he drank I kept my eyes moving. If that outlaw was somewhere about I had better see him before he saw me.

Cotton came from the overhang to call me, and saw me with the strange horse. He glanced at the brand, always the first thing any cowhand would do, and when I led the horse to tie him alongside our mounts, I told Cotton what I'd found.

"You still think Tarlton's around?" he asked.

"That could have been him who got away with the other horse."

We considered the question while we ate and drank coffee. Tarlton must be found. "He's a tough man, Cotton," I said. "I can read the sign. He's a gentleman, but there's iron in him, and he'll make a fight of it."

Leaving Cotton to guard the horses, I began a careful scout through the rain-drenched trees. Every branch I brushed sent down a shower of big drops. I found the second man in a nest of boulders and brush. He was dead, sprawled over a log behind which he had taken shelter. He had been shot through the skull, evidently as he was about to fire over the log. His rifle was there, his body as it must have fallen. The leaves under the body were dry.

Standing up, I looked in the direction which he must have faced. The man at whom he was about to fire must have been among the trees not far off. I walked ahead, making no sound upon the grass.

Two brass cartridge shells marked the place from which the man—Tarlton I hoped—had fired. There were no tracks a man could see, but a quick swing through the trees behind his firing position brought me to a barely discernible boot track, and then to the tracks of a horse.

I went back to Madden, and we mounted up and took

the trail. "He just backed out of the place and got away on his horse," I said. "I doubt if he knew his man was dead. He left the other horse, in case. Or maybe he was getting away with one horse when the other man opened up on him."

The hillside was slippery with mud. We found water standing in a well-defined track.

"He surely ain't ridin' for Cheyenne or Laramie," Cotton commented.

"He lost some cows, Cotton. He's going after them."

"Alone?"

"He's that kind of man. By the time he could get help those cattle might have been drifted miles away— even down into Colorado, maybe. He's riding a hot trail."

"How long ago, d'you figure?"

"Well, look at it. Caxton Kelsey, Queenie, and the rest were in Fort Laramie, so they must have had to leave the cattle at the Forks and drive a small bunch in to sell."

"Then Tarlton might have reached the Forks while they were gone."

Of course, the owner of the ranch would be there, and any riders he might have. And if it was a hide-out for outlaws, some of them might be around.

We came up to the Forks at sundown. The ranch was a low-roofed log shack about thirty feet long by ten feet wide, facing three large corrals and a lean-to shed, built on the flat between two creeks. The high banks of one of the creeks formed two sides of a still larger pasture on the bench beside the creek. It had been fenced at the upper and lower sides, and in the space between were several hundred head of cattle.

In the corral were at least two dozen horses. Cotton Madden studied the scene on the lower ground, then began to build a smoke. As he rolled the cigarette, we could see a slow column of smoke rising from the chimney below. A light appeared in a window.

Hunkered down behind the crest of the hill, I sat with Cotton hiding his cigarette in his cupped palm, and watched the ranch buildings turn from gray to black, then merge into the night, leaving only the lights in the window showing. For a short time, against the red of the sky, we could see the thin gray column of smoke, but it vanished shortly after the first star appeared.

Down below us a door slammed and we heard voices, but at that distance, we could make out no words. How many were down there? There might be two, or two dozen.

And where was Tarlton? Was he dead back there on the Wyoming grass? Or was he somewhere about, watching those lights, as we were? Or was he, perhaps, a prisoner down there? I doubted that. If they found him, they'd kill him ... if they could.

"What you figurin' to do?" Cotton asked.

"I'm studying on it. The logical thing would be to slip down there, open the corral bars, and stampede their horses and then the cattle. We could have them well on the trail north before they ever got horses."

"They'd come a-huntin' you," Cotton said.

"I'll face that when the time comes. The thing is, where's Tarlton? I've got an idea he's somewhere about, contemplating the same sort of action we're studying. I wouldn't want to stampede those cattle right over him."

We waited a spell, giving them a chance to finish eating and get to playing poker with their boots off, maybe, or to crawl into their bunks.

"Cotton," I said finally, "I'm going down there and scatter their saddle stock from hell to breakfast. You hang your rope over a post on the upper fence and pull her down, then circle around and start the cattle running. Get them out on the flat. Get them started north if you can, and come daybreak try to bunch them a mite. I'll catch up and lend a hand."

He pushed his hat back on his head and rubbed out his second cigarette. "No, you don't," he said. "We're in this together. I signed on to ride for the brand; and where you go, I'm going. If there's any shootin' done, it will be down there by the house and I want my piece of it."

I won't say I wasn't pleased. Two of us could handle it down there better than one, only I'd hoped to keep him out of range. "All right," I said, "if you want to get a belly full of lead, come on."

We tightened our cinches and mounted up. I doubted if they were keeping any sort of watch, but they would be quick to react to any kind of trouble. Our plan was simple: we would ride down the corral bars, and stampede the horses. All of them, I hoped.

Once the horses were on the run, we would ride to the corral and cut the north fence and stampede the herd. We would start them up the creek to where it came down from the flat, and start them north.

It wasn't likely they would be expecting trouble, for this was a lonely, isolated area in which nobody had begun to settle as yet. North of us and south of us there were trails or stage routes, but through this region there was nothing, and no ranches anywhere around.

To the north and south there were several good markets for small bunches of cattle. To the north it was the forts and the Indian agents; to the south it was the mines.

The night was still. We walked our horses down the slope of the hill toward the creek, following no trail. We could smell the wood smoke now. At the back of the corrals we drew up and swung down. "You keep an eye on the door and the windows," I said. "I'll open the corrals."

Hunkered down behind some logs, Cotton made ready to argue with anybody who might take it into his head to come outside. Me, I walked along the corral toward the gate, and was so intent on opening it quietly that I overlooked something I should have noticed. Lifting the bar, I swung the gate open . . . and all hell broke loose.

They had rigged a weight to pull the gate shut when anybody let go of it; and fastened to the same line they had half a dozen tin cans of pebbles. When I pulled that gate open, the line tightened and all those loose pebbles rattled in the cans.

Inside the house a chair fell over and somebody swore. The next thing I knew, as I was propping the gate open the house door opened and light fell across the yard, putting me right in the spotlight. At the same instant, Cotton fired.

The bullet hit the door jamb and the man in the door sprang back, swearing. Cotton fired again and I heard a rattle of falling glass, and then I was around the corral, sprinting for the back of it.

Cotton was up, yelling at the horses, and we heard them start. A rush of hoofs, more yells and shots, and the horses exploded from the wide-open gate.

Somebody fired from the house, the light went out, and men burst from the door, scattering right and left. I hit the saddle on the run and felt my horse's muscles go taut as he leaped away. Cotton let out a wild Texas yell, and we skirted the corral, guns blazing at the men around the house, and then we were racing away up the draw toward the cattle.

Cotton ran his horse up the bluff by a trail we had spotted earlier, while I drew up in the deepest shadows under some trees and waited, counting the seconds it would take him to reach the other side. Suddenly I heard a screeching of wire. Something broke, and I yelled at the cattle and fired my six-gun.

From almost under my feet a man leaped up and fired, the gun blazing right in my face, so close my eyes were momentarily blinded and I felt the powder sting my cheeks. I slammed down with my gun barrel at the black object I took to be a head and felt it fall away under my gun barrel with a grunt of pain.

My horse lunged toward the path up which Cotton had gone, but even as he sprang that way I saw something dark race across the trail ahead of me. "Block the trail!" came a yell, and I turned the buckskin on a dime and went racing away.

There were bluffs on both sides near the ranch house, and no chance to go up either of them. The pasture fence blocked the way toward the cattle and Cotton, and the only way left was back down and past the house. There was no time to hesitate, and I took it on the run.

Somebody had relighted the lamp in the house and the door stood open, throwing its rectangle of light on the hard-packed ground between the house and the corrals. I crossed that stretch of ground with my horse running all out, heard the slam of six-gun shots against my eardrums, and saw a man leap to the door and swing up with a rifle. Dropping low alongside my bronc, Indian-fashion, I snapped a shot at him from under my horse's neck. . . . Snapped was right—the gun was empty!

Tugging myself back into the saddle, I saw the rifle stab the darkness with flame and, holding the reins in my teeth, I thumbed cartridges into my gun. There seemed but one possible chance, and I turned my horse downstream, skirting a stack of hay and plunging into the unknown darkness beyond.

My horse was going full tilt when we saw the fence. It was just a glimpse, the darker bars across the gray, and the buckskin did the only thing he could do . . . he jumped.

There was an instant of flight, then the buckskin hit, went to his knees, and sent me flying over his head. Instinctively I tucked in my head, and when I hit the dirt I landed on my shoulder and rolled over. Momentarily dazed, I lay still, unsure whether I was alive or not. Staggering up, I could see nothing of my horse.

From the house came a shout. "Go get him! He can't get away!"

There was the sound of running feet and, turning, I

plunged into the blackness where there had been trees along the stream, if memory served me right. Luckily, dazed though I was, I reached the trees. Instantly, I stopped.

They would be right behind me, and they knew the terrain and I did not, Desperately, I needed my rifle, but it was in the scabbard on my saddle. The six-shooter was all right, but I trusted myself better with a rifle, and was prepared to face anything with a Winchester in my hands.

There were perhaps seven or eight of them, to judge by their voices. Occasionally they called out, as they moved down toward the pasture fence. They assumed I did not want to let my position be known and would not risk a shot, and they were right. To have fired one shot would have been to draw fire from all their rifles. One shot might miss; it was unreasonable to suppose eight would.

Putting my hand behind me, I felt bushes, and to my left a tree. I eased back against it, and worked my way around it, placing my foot down gently at each step until I knew what lay beneath it.

As they came on, I managed to put thirty feet or so behind me, and was desperately hoping to find some place to hide. The night was still. The lower pasture they were coming toward was much like the upper. As they reached the fence where I had taken my spill, I came to the fence along the side toward the creek. My hand touched a bark-covered rail, felt for the space beneath it, and then I slipped through. The stream must be close now.

It was growing lighter now . . . the moon would be rising. Remembering how the stream had looked from the crest of the hill above, I recalled that the stream bed was all of fifty yards wide, but the stream itself not over five or six. That meant I would be fully exposed, a black figure moving across white sand; and without doubt a rifleman would be watching such an easy target.

If a body had been taking odds, my chances were about fifty to one to wind up a corpse. There were a lot of men out there with the idea of salting me down, and they had the guns to do it with. Otis Tom Chancy's time looked to be about up. Nevertheless, I figured to make them pay for their fun. I had me a good bit of ammunition and I could shoot . . . maybe not as well as some, but well enough. As a last resort, I had a bowie knife with a blade sharp enough to slice bone as if it was cheese.

Suddenly a voice spoke, not twenty feet off. "Bud? I figure he got away. Plumb and total."

"You just hold that. You stow that gab. He didn't get away. There's no place he could go."

Looking past the two who spoke, I could see the dim figures of two or three men out in the pasture. Suddenly I had an idea. With those two there close by, I wasn't going to get away, but if—

Straightening up, I took careful aim at the little knot of figures out there, and fired.

Instantly, I dropped to my belly in the grass. It was as I'd figured. Those men out there in the pasture didn't stop to ask questions—somebody had shot at them and they shot back, all of them, and they kept on shooting. I got up and legged it out of there, running eight or ten steps before I slid down a bank and ran up a slight cut toward the cabin and the corrals.

Somebody back there was yelling. "Don't shoot, damn it! You've got Pike!"

Thumbing a shell into my gun, I came up out of the little draw, crossed behind the cabin, and started for the hills. It looked as if I was going to make it.

But all of a sudden a bunch of riders, unheard by me because of the shooting and yelling behind me, came down the trail to the cabin, right toward me.

There was no place to go. I was caught dead to rights, fair in the middle of the trail, with the moon just showing over the ridge. And my gun was in my holster. . . .

The riders drew up when they saw me from a distance. "Pike, what the hell's going on out there?"

It was Caxton Kelsey.

10

Kelsey had mistaken me for the man called Pike, and this gave me the break I needed. My holster was set for a crossdraw, and my right hand was at my belt. Moving it over, I shucked my gun, the darkness of my body masking the movement.

"Kelsey," I said, "I've got a gun lined on your belly. I've heard you're a fast man, but I don't think you are fast enough to beat a bullet."

He never moved. He was no fool, and he was not one to gamble against a sure thing. Nor were the others. They sat very still, every one. But you know who worried me the most? It was that red-headed woman, Queenie. A man you can figure on; a woman you can't. They're likely either to faint, or to grab for a gun regardless of consequences.

"It's you they're after, then." Kelsey drew on his cigarette and made it glow red in the night. "We'll get you this time. You're afoot."

"Not any more, Kelsey. I'm riding out of here right now. I'm riding your black. I'm not inclined to shoot

111

unless called upon, but at this range I should get two
or three of you, including the girl there."

Now, you hear about men arguing in the face of a
gun, or taking wild chances, but it is a rare thing that
you find a gun fighter gambling like that—he knows
too much about guns. By now I was within fifteen feet
of them, and just out of line of their horses.

"You could start shooting, or I could," I said, "and
I'd dearly love to put lead into you, Kelsey; but the way
I figure it, whoever starts shooting gets killed, and somebody else as well, maybe all of us. I don't like the odds,
but I don't have a choice. You boys do."

"What do you want us to do?"

"Let go your gunbelts. Just unloose the buckles and
let them fall. And when you've done that, shuck your
rifles and drop them."

"Cax, you ain't going to let him get away with this,
are you?" It was Queenie, and she was mighty angry—
ready to spit and snarl and scratch, given chance.

"Queenie," Kelsey said, cool and quiet, "you make
one wrong move and I'll kill you myself. This man
means business, and he's got nothing to lose." He
chuckled a little. "Besides, I like his nerve. It will be
real fun next time we meet when I gut-shoot him."

They unloosed their belts and let them fall, then
dropped their rifles.

"Now back up the length of your horses," I said,
"and get down from your saddles one at a time, Kelsey
first."

Nobody wanted to be a dead hero, and they did just
as I said. When they were all down, I told Kelsey to
lead his horse up to me. "Now, Kelsey, you be kinda
careful," I said. "I wouldn't want you to try to get that
horse between us, and if anything goes wrong I'm going
to kill you first . . . and you were the one who suggested
gut-shooting."

When I had the black, I rode over, starting their own
horses moving ahead of me toward the high range.

When Kelsey and his lot started down the trail, I

took time to swing down and gather up a rifle and a cartridge belt. I slung the extra belt over my shoulders and gathered up the others. Then swinging back into the saddle, I started up the trail, shucking shells from the belts as I rode, and stuffing them into my pockets.

Kelsey and the others were yelling, trying to draw some attention from the outfit at the ranch.

The black was a good horse and stepped right out, although he had come a far piece that day. Up on the high ground I glanced back; only the light from the ranch house showed. I kept to the west, testing the night for the smell of dust, which would mark the way taken by the stampeding herd.

Dawn was reaching red fingers at the sky when the smell of dust became strong, and I began coming up with scattered cattle. We started bunching them, the black and I, and he proved himself a good cow horse, with a liking for his job. Ranging back and forth in the growing light, we gathered strays and pushed them on to join the herd.

Cotton was out there, bringing up the drag. He swore with relief when he saw me. "Man, I thought you'd caught one! And my pony's durned near wore out with pushing this bunch."

"Keep right on pushing," I said. "We're heading for Cheyenne."

There was an idea buzzing in my head. They'd figure we would start for Fort Laramie, and might cut corners trying to head us off—when and if they got horses. If they followed our trail, it was a cinch they'd find us, but I had an idea Kelsey would be impatient to come up with us before we reached Fort Laramie.

We drove on into the dawning, and when day was full upon us, stopped for water.

Five of the Gates horses, stolen by the Kelsey outfit, were found among the cattle. They must have joined the herd in the night, knowing the cattle, and had trailed along. We roped them out, and felt better about the hard work ahead, but neither of us was of any mind to talk. Handy Corbin was still missing, and we had not found Tarlton.

There is something about a morning in the sagebrush country, something about the smell of leather and cows and horses, something about the smoke of a fire on the prairie, of coffee boiling and bacon frying . . . tired as I was—and believe me, every muscle and bone in my body ached—I loved it.

"Wonder how the boys are makin' out back at the ranch," Cotton Madden said suddenly. "I really do miss ol' Tom. He's been like a daddy to me . . . not that he's that much older, only he's been a man grown ever since I first knowed him."

"He's a good man. They're both good men."

"You're from Tennessee?" Cotton asked.

"Cumberland country," I said, "but nobody's waiting for me back yonder."

He glanced at me. "You on the dodge?"

It was a question nobody asked out here, but I didn't take it wrong, coming as it did from Cotton Madden. So many men out here had left home for reasons of health.

"No," I said, "and there'll be a time when I go back. There's some folks I want to straighten out a mite."

Suddenly we heard a horse whinny, and you never saw two men roll out of sight so fast. But it was Buck, my buckskin, packing my gear. He'd come on our trail and followed it right along. I never was so glad to see a horse in my life, and it beats all how attached a man can get to a piece of horseflesh. Best of all, I had my outfit back, and my own rifle.

We hazed the cattle west and south, and the sage-brush levels fell away before us, or lifted in slow waves of hills, one no different from another. There was a reason for our dropping by Cheyenne, for we needed another cowhand—perhaps two if we were to drive this herd north. Moreover, there was a good chance that Tarlton would have gone there, if he was alive.

Cheyenne was in cattle country. The cattlemen had

started moving into the area several years before, and by this time they were well established. I'd find friends here, I knew.

It was a wild, wild town. It had been hell on wheels, the end of the track, and many of the saloons and gambling houses were still active. It was not a big place . . . at its biggest there had been several thousand people there, most of them passers-by, but the ones here now were about half passers-by and about half folks who were settled, or who planned to settle there.

Leaving Cotton with the cattle, I rode into town, and first off I saw a man with a star. Now, the man wearing the badge was usually a solid citizen, although sometimes he was an ex-outlaw. When I pulled up my horse, this one looked over at me and I swung down. He was a tall, well-setup man with a brown, drooping mustache. He was neatly dressed and carried himself with a confident air, yet without arrogance.

"Marshal," I said, "I'm with a cow outfit, and I need a couple or three cowhands. I want solid men who'll ride for the brand, no dead beats and no rustlers."

He took the cigar from his mouth. "I might find some men," he said. "Where you ranching?"

"We've just started," I answered. "We drove a herd into the Hole-in-the-Wall country a few months back."

He stared at me. "You must be crazy! That's right in the heart of Indian country."

"It's good grass, and there's water," I explained, "and when I left there'd been no Indian trouble. Only trouble we've had," I added, "was with Caxton Kelsey and his outfit."

That stopped him, as I expected it would. "Kelsey's at the Hole-in-the-Wall?"

"No, sir. He's riding for Laramie right now, or maybe trailing us here. He's got blood in his eye and he's hunting me."

So I gave him the whole story, right from the beginning, and he stood there and listened, chewing on his cigar, his eyes sweeping the street. It seemed to me that it was in Cheyenne the way it had been in Abilene, and if I wanted the law to understand my position I'd best tell my story first. If there was a gun battle he would have no choice but to treat both sides the same, unless he knew the real truth of the matter.

Kelsey's name helped. He was a known bad man—not only a bad man with a gun, but an outlaw. In those days, when you said somebody was a bad man you did not mean that he was necessarily an evil man. It might just mean that he was a bad man to tangle with. Kelsey was all of that, but he was more. LaSalle Prince had an even worse reputation, and Andy Miller was a bad one, too.

"When you pick your enemies," the marshal said, "you pick them tough."

"They picked me," I said. "I came to Wyoming to ranch, and if there's trouble it will be because they come riding to fetch it."

The marshal tipped his hatbrim down. "So happens," he said, "that I've got a lobster up there in my jail right about now that might be just the man you want."

"In jail?" I sounded skeptical.

"Don't worry. I wouldn't point you down the wrong trail. He's a good man." He grinned at me. "He's just full of cockleburs and sand, and he wants to fight everybody in town. But I happen to know that out on the range he's a first-class cowhand."

He reached into his pocket and took out a key. "He's over at the jail, and his name is Corky Burdette. He can ride anything that wears hair, and he'll fight anything that walks. You go let him out and tell him I said he was to go to work for you."

"Marshal, there's one more thing. Have you seen or heard anything of Bob Tarlton? Or Handy Corbin?"

"Tarlton's a cattle buyer, isn't he?"

"He was . . . he's my partner."

"Good reputation." He rolled his cigar in his lips. "I know Handy Corbin, too. What's he to you?"

"He works for me. He's a good hand."

"Yes, he is that." The marshal took his cigar from his mouth and glanced at me sharply. "Did you know he was a cousin to LaSalle Prince? They grew up together."

Well, you could have knocked me down with a pencil, I was that surprised. I could only shake my head. Corbin had said nothing about knowing Prince. In fact, he had not said anything about himself at all, nor had I expected it.

The marshal turned away. "If I see them, I'll let them know you're in town." And he walked away down the street.

The jail had a cubbyhole of an outer room, with a desk and a chair, and a saddle thrown into one corner. There were two cells, each with four bunks, and Corky Burdette was seated on a bunk in one of the cells, riffling a deck of worn cards.

He was a square-jawed man, and I found that he had a blunt, whimsical way about him. He glanced up at me. "The marshal is out," he said. "If you want to leave a message, just whistle it and I'll try to remember the tune."

"I met him up the street. He said you were a good hand with stock, as well as a peaceful, contented man."

"I'll bet he did. What else did he say?"

"That you were to go to work for me." I held up the key. "He also gave me this."

"Work for you? The hell I will! When I get out of here I'm going to look up a guy I know, and—"

"Why waste your time fighting around here? Come with me and you can do something besides beating up sod-busters."

"What if I don't work for you?"

I shrugged. "In that case I throw the key away. The nearest locksmith is in Denver, and it would take a few weeks to get word down there, get that locksmith sobered up, and talk him into making a new key. Then it would have to be brought back here from Denver. Of course, Indians might lay for the man bringing the key, and it might get lost. In which case they'd have to go back down to Denver, find the locksmith, sober him up—"

"All right, all right! I can read sign as well as you, mister. Where's your outfit?"

"Up in the Hole-in-the-Wall country."

"*What?* Are you off your rocker? A man could get himself killed up there."

"You scared?" I said. "Are you a fighter, or just a Saturday night drunk?"

He came off the bunk. "Open that door and I'll show you!"

"You?" I sneered at him. "Why, I'd pin back your ears, grease your hair, and swallow you whole. If you ever take a punch at me I'll bounce you so high they'd have to shoot you to keep you from starving to death."

He chuckled suddenly. "Open the door, boss, you've hired yourself a boy."

Once outside the cell, he took his gun belt and rifle from a hook behind the door, and shouldered the saddle.

"Let's go eat," I said, "and I'll lay it out for you. Then if you want to call it off, you can."

We were sitting over coffee when the marshal came in. "Chancy, I found your man."

"Tarlton?"

"He's over at the Doc's office, and he's in pretty bad shape. A rider brought him in just before daybreak. He'd been shot a couple of times, and he'd dragged himself a good ways. You'd better get on over there."

We got up and I dropped money on the table to pay for our meal, then as the marshal reached the door, I asked, "Who was the man who brought him in? Do you know him?"

"He didn't give his name. He was a man with a tied-down gun . . . sounded like Handy Corbin."

We followed the marshal out the door and he pointed to indicate the Doc's office. Nothing in this town was very far away. If you walked a hundred yards in any direction you'd be out on the prairie.

Corky Burdette walked along beside me. "This Corbin . . . do you know him?"

"He works for me."

"Then you've got a good man," Corky said, "a mighty good man. We worked for the same outfit back in the Nation, and again down Texas way."

I found Tarlton drawn and pale. A stubble of reddish beard covered his cheeks, although I'd thought of him as a dark-haired man. He was asleep when we came in.

"How bad is he, Doc?" I asked.

"He's got a fighting chance. The wounds wouldn't have been so bad if they'd been cared for. But they've become infected, and he's lost a lot of blood, as well as suffered from exposure and physical exhaustion."

We left and rode out to the herd. The cattle were grazing on good grass, and seemed content. Cotton came to meet us with a rifle across his saddle.

"Keep your eyes open," I warned. "Kelsey might show up any time." Then I asked Cotton, "Did Handy ever say anything to you about being kin to LaSalle Prince?"

"Now, that don't make sense. We talked about Prince, but he never said anything about even knowing him. Seemed to me he didn't set much store by him. . . . I sort of figured he'd just heard of him, like I have."

Corky took first guard, and I rolled up in my blankets. I'd been on my feet or in the saddle for about twenty hours, and I was dead tired. I told him to call me for the next turn.

When he came in and shook me awake, I could see by the stars that he had let me sleep over my time by a good hour or more. "I was goin' to let you sleep right on through," he admitted, "only I just got too durned sleepy."

He stood by while I tugged on my boots and had my coffee, and all the while kept listening toward the cattle. "There's something out there," he said in a minute, and he gestured toward the brush along the creek. "I figure it's a varmint of some kind. The critters can smell it, and they're spooky."

When I was in the saddle, he added, "You watch that ol' blaze-face mossy-horn on the far side. He's got it in his head to run."

"I know him," I said. "He's a trouble-maker. Next time the Indians come around hunting beef they're going to get him."

Now, a body never knows when he starts out to do something just what will come of it, else maybe nothing would ever get done. That night I was riding a hammer-headed roan that had belonged to the Gates outfit, and I headed for the herd and started to sing to 'em.

So far as I know there's some Welsh as well as Irish blood in me, but when they were handing out the good voices they surely didn't allow me to take after most Welshmen. I couldn't carry a tune in a hand-basket. Maybe that's one reason I like cows—they're got no ear for music.

So I started out singing "Peter Grey," "Skip to My Lou," and "Buffalo Gals." I made it around the herd a few times, singing soft and low, keeping an eye on that mossy-horn with the cross-grained notions in his head.

By the time I had ridden three times around the herd I knew Corky Burdette had been right. That old mossy-horn was going to make trouble, and not for the first time. He had always been a bunch-quitter, for he had been one of the original Gates herd, stolen by the Kelsey outfit, and I knew him well.

Whatever had been out there in the brush was gone now, and the rest of the cattle were settling down, but not that blaze-faced steer. He was prodding around, just hunting something to be scared of, so's he could take off and run, stampeding the lot of them.

There's times when any little noise will startle a herd into running, but those cattle knew me and they knew my horse, and I had an idea they wouldn't be too upset if there was a little fussing around where I was. So I decided to side-line the mossy-horn before he could get the herd to spill over into a stampede.

Actually, I wasn't about to side-line him, but I figured to tie his head down to his foreleg to persuade him he didn't want to run. My intentions were good, and the steer would suffer no harm from having his neck canted over a bit; but a body can't always have things the way he figures, and I was doing my figuring without remembering the horse I was on.

When I skirted the herd again, I dabbed a loop on that old steer and busted him, but just as I hit the ground to make my tie, that cantankerous, rattle-brained pony I'd been riding slacked up on the rope and the steer came for me, head down.

Now, a steer can bust a man considerable, so as he charged I grabbed for my gun and came up with it, but a mite too slow. Luckily, using the cross-draw I'd turned my left hip toward my right hand, and the steer hit me only a glancing blow. I went right over his horns and into the dirt, and my six-gun went a-flying.

My mouth and eyes scraped dirt and I rolled over, frantic to get away from the steer, and came up to my knees just in time to see him start back at me. Only this time that darned fool pony, scared now, started toward him and busted the mossy-horn right over on his back.

Coughing and spitting, fighting the dirt from my eyes, I looked around for my gun. It was nowhere in sight. Dark as it was, I knew I'd play hob trying to find it until daybreak, so I edged around toward camp.

The rest of the herd didn't seem much bothered. They were well-fed, freshly watered, and bedded down in a good spot, and only a few of them that were nearby even showed interest. Me, I limped for camp.

Cotton was sitting up when I walked in. "What happened to you?" he asked.

He chuckled when I explained. "Wait up. It's time for me to take over, anyway, and I'll saddle up and collect them."

We went back out together and he caught up my

horse. The rope was still on the steer, which was backed off at the end of the rope, staring at us. I got into the saddle and Cotton eased around and put another rope on the steer, and we threw him and tied his head down. He would be of no mind to run now; and a few days of that would take some of the vinegar out of him. Back at camp again, I went to sleep.

Corky was up and putting together some bacon and eggs when I opened my eyes. He grinned at me. "Hear you went around and around with that old mossy-horn," he said. "Well, it happens to the best of us."

"It sure happened to me," I said. "He really tossed me."

As I started to swing my gunbelt into place, I noticed the empty holster. "Lost my gun," I said. "Keep an eye out for it, will you?"

Not liking the feel of the empty holster, I dug into my pack and came up with the ivory-handled gun I'd taken off that would-be sheriff back in the Nation. It was a fine gun, one of the best I'd seen, with a great feel to it. I checked the load, then dropped it into my holster.

"Carry a spare, do you?" Corky said.

"Picked it up back in the Nation," I answered. "It'll do until I find my own. I feel naked without a gun."

Bacon and eggs was a rare treat for a cowhand, and about the only time we ever got anything of the kind was when we were close to town, as we were now to Cheyenne. They tasted almighty good and I could see that Corky was a hand with a skillet as well as with his fists.

"You riding into town?" he asked presently.

"Uh-huh."

"Look," he said, "the one thing I wanted in Cheyenne was some canned peaches or pears, or something like that. I get fed up with this grub. How about picking up a few cans for me?"

"For us," I said. "I like 'em, too."

And that's just the way hell builds a trap for a man;

for between that ornery, no-account steer and a few cans of peaches, I was riding right into trouble—more trouble than I'd ever had in my life.

Mainly I was riding in to see how Tarlton was coming on. It was time to be heading back up to the Hole-in-the-Wall country, and I felt we couldn't wait. The last thing I wanted was more trouble than I had, but the past has a way of catching up with a man, and right there in Cheyenne it was about to catch up to me.

11

Puffed-up clouds like woolly sheep grazed on the pasture of the sky when I rode into Cheyenne. The wind skittered a few dry leaves ahead of me, and occasionally a gust whipped my horse's tail against the heels of my boots or the saddle leather. I was riding proud, for it was that kind of a morning, and the air was fresh and cool off the mountains.

Up on a balcony a man was washing a window of the hotel when I came up the street, riding abreast of my own dust. He glanced down at me, and I went on toward the Doc's office and dismounted at the door.

Doc was at his roll-top desk with a heavy white cup and saucer at his hand. The cup was filled with steaming coffee, and it smelled good to me after my ride. Open before him on the desk was an old ledger in which he was entering accounts, peering at them unhappily through gold-rimmed glasses. Glancing around, he recognized me and jerked a thumb toward the inner room. "He's awake. Go on in."

It seemed to me that as he started to turn back to

his ledger he did a sudden look-back at me, but, eager to see Tarlton, I went on inside.

Bob was sitting up in bed, and he had been reading. Putting the book aside, he held out his hand. "I never was so glad to see anybody in my life, Chancy! You're looking great."

"Can't say the same of you, but you're shaping up a sight better then when I last saw you."

"Have you seen Corbin? He brought me in."

"No, I haven't seen him," I said, "and we could surely use him. I've hired another hand—seems like a good man."

"We never had a chance, Otis. Those boys came on us right out of nowhere in what looked like open country. They stampeded our cattle, and killed two of my boys before we ever knew what hit us. We were scattered out, and there was no place to get down and make a stand. Their first fire wounded me, and when my horse went down I lost my sixshooter. I made a stand with my rifle—"

"We found the place."

"They circled, too far out. I couldn't get a good shot at them, so they just drove off the cattle and left me there. They knew I was wounded, had no horse, and was without water, and they probably decided I was as good as dead."

"We picked up your sign. You trailed them."

"They had our cattle. I trailed them as far as I could, and after I'd passed out, Handy Corbin found me and brought me in here."

We heard the outer door slam, and Tarlton made a sudden move to rise.

"Damn it," he said, "Doc was going to mail a letter on the noon stage for me. I wonder what got him started off like that?" He glanced at me. "I wanted to let my family know where I am. Have you got any family, Otis?"

"No, I surely haven't. Not close-up kin, leastways. I'm related to the Sacketts. There's a passel of them out

in this western country, but they don't know me, nor
I them."

We sat there talking, and it was pleasant. Outside a
chilly wind was picking up, but in here it was cozy,
and I liked Bob Tarlton. To a man who'd never had a
real friend before, he seemed like one. He talked of
his folks and his home in the East, it was a life I'd
never known, nor was I likely to. It was all a far-off
thing, remote from these dusty plains, and it seemed
farther still from the mountain villages I'd known in
Tennessee. It was a genteel life, lived among folks who
wore white shirts and black suits, who rode in shining
carriages and talked business over coffee and cigars.
I'd seen a few pictures of folks like that in magazines,
time to time, but I could never figure what they did for
a living, if anything.

Bob Tarlton knew that world, and he talked of
college, and business, and shooting ducks for sport, of
walking with girls in a park of a Sunday, listening to
band concerts and the like. Me, I just sat there turning my hat in my hand, thinking that those stories were
like some kind of magic, making me realize there was
a world I wanted to understand, and someday to know,
myself.

Back in the hills in Tennessee we had no really rich
folks, except for Martin Brimstead, and very few that
could be called well-off, except maybe the Dunvegans
before I'd wrecked their world. All I knew were horses,
cattle, and guns, and I had some memories of knocking
around here and there as a boy after I'd left the mountains. I'd seen some eastern towns, but only from the
waterfront side, which is no way to judge any place.

While I sat there with these thoughts in my mind,
Tarlton finally got sleepy, so I excused myself and went
down the street to get those cans of fruit Corky wanted.
Despite the fact that it was chilly, a good many folks
were out on the street, and most of them seemed to be
just standing talking. When I came along they turned
their heads to watch me, and I got a jumpy feeling, as

if something was wrong—I wondered if maybe Caxton Kelsey was in town with his outfit.

At the store, folks kind of stood aside for me. I went to the counter and ordered cans of peaches, plums, and pears. The store had the good smell of drygoods, leather, dried fruit, and such things. There was never any smell so good as the smell of a general store, unless maybe that of a blacksmith shop with the forge working.

"Just put those cans in a gunny sack," I said. "I've a couple of cowboys a-hungering for them."

"They'll have to wait, then." It was the marshal's voice, and when I turned around he had a gun on me. "Lift your hands, Chancy," he said. "I'm taking your gun."

A dozen men had crowded into the door, all of them staring, mean as could be.

"What's the trouble, Marshal?" I kept my voice low, not wanting to excite anybody.

"Just unbuckle your belt, Chancy. I'd not like to kill a man in cold blood, no matter what kind of a coyote he is."

The storekeeper was behind me to my left. There was no room to try anything, even if I'd been of a mind to start a gun battle in a room crowded with innocent folk. Besides, this just had to be a mistake.

"That's strong talk, Marshal, and you holding a gun on me. What do you want me for? I've done nothing."

"How about back in the Nation?" The speaker was a big burly man with prominent blue eyes and a red face. "What kind of a chance did you give Burgess?"

There was something I couldn't figure out, something missing. "I don't know any Burgess," I said.

"Then where did you get that gun? You're wearing Burgess' gun, and ever'body around here knows it."

It didn't take any fortune-teller to tell me I was in trouble. Those folks were mad, and most of them had the look of being good men, too. Even the marshal, to whom I'd talked friendly, had no friendly look for me now. And here I stood, a lone man with nobody to stand beside me or to speak a word for me.

"I took this gun off a man who tried to cut our herd back yonder. He was a no-account, posing as a sheriff."

The red-faced man pushed forward. "Burgess *was* a sheriff, and he was a damned good man! Marshal, how long you going to stand there talking? I say we take him out and hang him."

"Take it easy, Weber. Just keep your shirt on." The marshal measured me coldly. "Where did all of this happen, Chancy? Where were you?"

"It was back in the Cherokee Nation. I'd just come down out of Tennessee and had come up to this herd . . . Noah Gate's outfit. They'd had trouble with some herd-cutters, led by a man posing as a sheriff and wearing a badge. I bought in with them, and when this man tried to run a bluff and drew on me, I killed him. He was wearing this gun."

"Alec Burgess wasn't that kind of man," somebody else was saying. "He was decent and law-abiding. Moreover, he was a dead shot with either hand. You'd play hell killing him unless you dry-gulched him."

"You've got witnesses, I suppose?" the marshal suggested to me.

That stopped me. For there were no witnesses any more, none but Queenie, and she would take delight in lying to get me hung. "Noah Gates and his outfit were the only witnesses. They are dead . . . all of them, so far as I know."

"Then there isn't even one witness?"

"Marshal, the only person alive who could testify to what happened is Queenie, that red-headed daughter-in-law to Noah Gates, but she's running with the wild bunch, the same outfit I've been hunting. And she'd swear me into hell any time she got a chance."

"Drop your gunbelt, Chancy," the marshal said. "I'm taking you in."

"Will I get a trial?"

"A trial?" the red-faced man sneered. "You don't

deserve any more of a trial than you gave Burgess. Why wait, Marshal? I've got a rope in my wagon. Let's string him up!"

There were several shouts of agreement, but the marshal turned quickly around. "There'll be none of that," he said sternly. "All right, Chancy. Drop your belt or I'll shoot."

With careful fingers, I unbuckled, and there was a sinking in me when I did it. What chance was I going to have? I didn't know any Burgess, nor even where the crime was supposed to have happened, nor how. But I had no witnesses, no defense, and it had happened somewhere back in the Territory or the Nation, and I had been there at the time.

Of only one thing could I be sure. The man of whom they talked, this Alec Burgess, could not have been the man I killed, but how could I prove that? I had been accused and arrested simply because I wore a dead man's gun.

With the crowd following behind, the marshal took me down to the jail and locked me in the same cell from which I had released Corky Burdette.

When that barred door slammed shut, I just dropped down on the bunk and stared blankly, too stunned to think about what had happened to me. From the muttering of the men outside I had an idea it wasn't over . . . and all because of picking up a dead man's gun.

Bob Tarlton was sick in bed, and was not likely to hear of what had happened to me. The boys were out at the herd, and just standing guard over those cows would keep them busy. There was nobody around anywhere to whom I could look for help. But then, I had never been one to expect help. That's one advantage of always being a loner, you've just got to do it yourself . . . whatever has to be done.

The worst of it was, I didn't even know what had happened. Seemed as if this Alec Burgess had been a well-thought-of man, and he'd gone east and been murdered. Well, that man I'd killed back there seemed a likely one to have done such a thing, but was he? After all, Burgess was some shakes with a gun, they said, and that would-be sheriff wasn't a man to buck anything like that. A dry-gulch, maybe . . . and they'd as much as said that was the way it was. Still, there must have been more to it.

The marshal had gone back to his desk and seated himself, his rifle lying across the desk in front of him. Then he began shuffling through some old "Wanted" posters.

There was one window in the cell, with three iron bars. From the way the jail building stood, that window must look out on open country. Crow Creek was out there somewhere, and there was brush along the creek, and trees. How long would it take a man to cover that distance if he was out of here?

"Don't you get to thinkin' you can break out of here," the marshal said from behind me. "Those boys would hang you to the nearest tree right off. They thought a lot of Alec."

"Look," I said, "no matter what bee you've got in your bonnet, I had nothing to do with killing this Alec Burgess. I took that gun off a would-be sheriff . . . probably the very star he was sporting came off Burgess. I lost my gun last night, so I dug this one out of my blanket roll. Now, if I'm going to be accused of murdering a man you might at least tell me something about what happened."

His eyes searched mine, and then, reluctantly, he said, "You know better than me. All we know is that Burgess and four other men started for Fort Smith, escorting a wagon with a woman and her husband in it, and two prisoners who were riding the wagon.

"Nobody heard nothing of Burgess and the others, and then their bodies were found. The prisoners were gone, cut loose. Burgess and the others had been ambushed, all of them killed, including the woman.

Finding this gun was the first clue we've come across, but everybody will want your scalp now."

There was nothing in what he had told me that was of any help, but I could understand the feelings of the men who wished to hang me. A well-liked man had been killed, too. But it must have taken more than one man to bring it off, and they must have had a strong motive to try it.

"Who were the prisoners?" I asked.

"Hood Cuyler and Rad Miller."

"Rad Miller!" I came off the bed with a lunge that made the marshal step back from the bars. "Miller was one of the rustlers we've had trouble with! Do you think I'd risk my neck to help him get free?"

"I thought of that, but you might have had a falling out since. Or your whole story may be a pack of lies."

"Rad Miller is dead. I killed him out on the plains when he was chasing one of the Gates outfit. Handy Corbin can tell you that, so can Cotton Madden."

"That's another thing," the marshal said calmly. "Handy Corbin is related to Prince, and we have reason to believe Prince was in on that deal."

"It doesn't make sense. When we had the run-in with that would-be sheriff we'd never met up with Kelsey's outfit."

The marshal shrugged. "No? You told me they'd been following the herd . . . that Kelsey was playing patty-cake with Gates's daughter-in-law. How do you know there wasn't some tie-up?"

Of course, I did not know . . . could not know. In my mind they had been separate incidents, and I could not get rid of the notion. Still, that did not mean there mightn't have been a tie-up. If the Kelsey outfit wanted to deliver Rad Miller, they might recruit help from anybody likely to take a hand . . . and that bunch there where the would-be sheriff tried to cut our herd had been a pack of outlaws.

None of this was likely to do me any good. Folks out west, where there was only occasionally some kind of organized law, had a way of taking justice in their own hands on the least excuse. My neck would probably be stretched before anybody knew I was the wrong man . . . if they would ever know.

Somehow, some way, I had to get out of this place.

The marshal left me, and I was alone. The sun was warm outside . . . I worried about my horse, left standing at the hitching rail. I got up and tried the door. It was securely locked. The window bars were set solidly. From up the street I could occasionally hear laughter, the clink of glass, the rattle of a pump at a well, or the slam of a door.

After a while I stretched out on my bunk to consider the situation. There had to be a way out, and I'm a man who has always believed that a man can think his way out of most things if he'll only try hard enough. But no ideas came to me, and presently I fell asleep. When I awoke it was cooler, the sun was far down the sky . . . night was coming.

And nighttime meant trouble. Men would be free from their work, they would gather in the saloons to discuss my case, and they would start drinking. I knew very well what a drunken mob could be like. From the barred door I could look across the office and out through a front window. All I could see was dust, brown grass, and the edge of a building.

Gripping the bars of the door, I stared out through the window. I was scared. Was I going to be strung up for something I had not done? Ending on a rope, as pa had done?

My gunbelt and rifle were yonder in the corner of the office, the ivory-handled pistol still in its holster. They might have been ten miles away, for all the good they could do me.

Up the street the tin-panny music box started once more. Two men rode along, and dust drifted from their passing. I paced the narrow cell.

Suppose I did break out? They'd think me guilty for certain then. But if I stayed they might string me up, and they would never even know they'd done a wrong thing. I hadn't any idea what I should do . . . or could do.

I tried lying down on my bunk again, but I couldn't sleep. Sitting up once more, I studied the matter. I had to get out and away—I couldn't just sit here until they came after me.

But what about the marshal? Would he stand by and let it happen? He did not seem the type. I had him figured for a good man, a solid man, who would stand four-square for what he believed . . . but he was only one man.

Slowly my eyes ran around the room. The place was solidly built. There wasn't so much as a crack I could get a finger into. I was locked in, tight as a sardine in a can.

Out on the street, somebody whooped drunkenly. It was beginning now . . . how long before they came for me?

12

Suddenly I heard the sound of horses' hoofs, and looking out through the office window, I could see several riders coming into town. As they passed by, I saw that they were Caxton Kelsey, LaSalle Prince, Andy Miller, Queenie, and at least two others.

They rode on by, into the town's street. Now what was that about? Why would they risk coming here now? Or had they heard of my arrest? I asked that question of myself, then decided against it as too unlikely. They must have another reason, probably nothing more than a chance for a few drinks, a chance to buck a faro game.

I paced the floor of my cell. If only I was free now, with a gun in my hand! But even if I was free, what could I do that would clear me of the charge against me? Queenie hated me, and she would cheerfully see me hang; and undoubtedly the others felt the same. Anyway, I didn't want to be free if I had to leave this charge behind.

So what to do? It always came back to that. I was here, a mob was undoubtedly forming up the street, and

I had no idea whether the marshal would make an effort to stop them or not.

There was no chance of getting a message out. No one even came close to the jail—the area around it was empty.

Lights were coming on in the town. A long, low wind stirred the sage, bringing the wild, free smell of it to my nostrils.

Was this the way it was going to end after all my dreams? After all my hopes of returning to face those who had killed my father? Was I to end as he had?

Feverishly, I searched my cell again . . . there *had* to be a way out! I shook the bars of the door, but they were solid. I tried the bars of the window again, as I had before, and they, too, were firm.

Somewhere along the line I must have dozed. I recall sitting down on the bunk and stretching out. The next thing I knew I was awake. It was still dark; outside I could hear a murmur, as of somebody talking.

I got up quickly. Lights still showed bright in the town, and somewhere I heard a wild yell, then a smashing of glass, and coarse laughter. A rider went by, riding fast.

Then I heard footsteps—somebody was coming toward the jail at a fast walk. The door opened, and I saw a body bulk briefly against the lights of the town, then the door closed.

"Chancy?" It was the marshal. "You awake?"

"You think I could sleep with that crowd liquoring up over there?"

But I had been asleep, and I wondered for a moment how I could have relaxed that much. "Are they coming?" I asked.

"They're talking," he said. "Maybe it's all talk."

"Are you going to let me have a gun?"

He considered that, while I could have counted a slow ten. "Maybe," he said, "if it comes to that. Nobody's ever taken a prisoner from me, and nobody is going to."

"I never killed Alec Burgess," I told him again, "or even saw him. I'll state that for a fact, and I'm not a lying man."

"Who are you, Chancy?" I couldn't even see him clearly there in the dark, but I could see he held a rifle and was watching out the window.

"Who?" Well, who was I, after all? "I'm nobody," I said. "I'm a mountain boy who never had much but his health, some ugly memories, and a hope for the future. Back yonder," I said, "they hung my pa for a horse thief, and a better man never lived. He wasn't tough or mean; he was a mighty good man."

Sitting there in the darkness of the jail, I told the marshal about pa, and the horse business and the hanging.

"I've always wanted to go back there," I said. "I've wanted to go back there and show 'em."

"They tell me you can use a gun."

"I don't want to use one in Tennessee. There isn't anybody, anywhere, I'd want to kill. I just want to go back there and show them I've made good . . . and here I am about to get my neck stretched."

Just then we heard footsteps. They were slow, halting steps. A hand touched the latch, but the door was locked.

"Marshal? Are you in there? Open up . . . this is Bob Tarlton."

The marshal opened the door, and Bob got himself through the door. He was walking with a cane, and carrying a rifle in his free hand.

"Chancy? Are you there?" he said.

"I'm here—and you ought to be back there in bed."

He dropped into the marshal's chair, and I could hear his ragged breathing. "Let him out, Marshal." He spoke with an effort. "I'll stand good for him."

After a moment's hesitation, the marshal unlocked the cell door. Crossing to the corner, I picked up my gun belt and slung it about my hips, then I took up the rifle. It was dark in the room, our eyes had grown accustomed to the darkness, and we could dimly make out one another.

"One thing," I said: "that girl Queenie is in town. She could tell the truth about this if she would. She's got no use for me, but she was there when I killed that man who was packing this gun. She saw it happen."

Nobody said anything. We could hear the shouts from the town, and then the sound of a door slamming. We could hear them coming, stumbling and swearing. These were the riffraff—drifters, no-accounts. I knew the type, for I had seen them before, many of them good enough men when sober, but now as a mob they were beyond reasoning, thinking only of a good man gone, and a prisoner who might get away with it.

"Why don't you two leave?" I suggested. "It's me they want."

"We're partners," Tarlton said. "Remember?"

The marshal made no reply; he merely opened the window and closed the heavy shutters, and then opened a loophole in the shutter.

"All right, out there!" he shouted. "Turn right around and go back! There'll be no lynching tonight!"

They kept coming, and he fired into the ground, well ahead of them. "Back up, now!" he said loudly. "I'm not alone, and if you want a fight you can have it."

They stopped and stood there in the darkness, a tight knot of men, muttering among themselves.

"Turn him out, Marshal!" one man called. "Turn him out and we'll give him what he's got coming!"

"Not tonight you won't!" It was another voice, speaking from the roof top. "I'm up here with a Colt repeatin' shotgun, an' I can cut your front rank down with my first two shots!"

It was Handy Corbin—I would have known his voice anywhere. He must have brought my shotgun from camp. And he was right: at that range that shotgun would kill or maim half a dozen at each firing. It didn't carry bird shot, but buckshot of .38 caliber.

Bob Tarlton stood up and opened the door. "Forget

it, boys. We don't want to hurt anybody, but we've got an open field of fire and you wouldn't have a chance."

Drunk as they were, they knew they were up against at least three men, maybe more. Muttering, they backed off. Some of those in the front rank began to ease off, trying to put other men in front of them. Those in the rear began drifting back toward the saloon. In a few minutes the space in front of the jail was empty.

The marshal lighted a lamp. Reluctantly, I laid my rifle on the table, then started to unbelt my pistol.

"Hold that," the marshal said. "You keep your rifle. I'll need that pistol for evidence."

"Thanks. There's a herd of cattle out yonder, and a long trail ahead of us. If you want me, I'll be at the Hole-in-the-Wall. You just come up there or send a messenger and I'll come down. . . . I'm not guilty of anything except defending a herd from bunch-cutters."

"You go ahead," the marshal said. "I believe you, but there'll have to be a hearing."

"The crime wasn't committed in your jurisdiction, Marshal," Tarlton said quietly, "and the story of that shooting was well known in Kansas. I'd heard it before I ever met Otis Tom Chancy."

We walked back toward the doctor's office together, and we had gone fifty yards before I remembered Handy Corbin. Letting go of Tarlton, I turned to go back, but there Corbin was, only a few yards behind us.

"You huntin' me?" he said. "I figured to trail along an' make sure you got home safe. You got enemies, boy."

"I know—I saw Kelsey and his crowd ride in."

We had reached the door of the doctor's office by then. Corbin grinned at me, but his eyes were serious. "I wasn't talking about them," he said; "I was referring to some other folks."

I couldn't figure out who he meant. He walked along a few steps and then said, "You know the railroad has men back east recruitin' settlers—dirt farmers, most of them. They've promised 'em big farms, rich soil . . .

land that's almost for the taking. Well, they've con-
vinced a lot of folks, and some of the crooked land
speculators have been back there, too.

"Why, they tell that whole villages have picked up
an' come west, just achin' to get rich. You ain't been
around Cheyenne much, but you can see trains come
in with fifty, sixty families getting off, all to once. An'
it's even worse in some places back along the line."

"What's that got to do with enemies of mine?" I
asked.

Corbin stopped and pushed his hat back. He started
to build a cigarette.

"Seems like some crackerjack salesman went into
the Tennessee country and fetched 'em such tales they
all packed up, bag an' baggage, to come west. I was
sort of perambulatin' around when they come in, and
heard some talk. Somebody mentioned that they
shouldn't be too anxious to leave town, not with a
hangin' to watch.

"Well, when they heard who was being hung, they all
swore they'd not want to miss seeing the boy hung,
when they'd helped hang his pa."

"Was one of them a big, burly man with a reddish
face?" I asked.

"A loud-mouth . . . but big and mean," Corbin said.

"Stud Pelly. Well, what about that? And I figured
I'd have to traipse all the way back to Tennessee to see
him."

We went into the doctor's office and helped Bob
Tarlton back into bed. By now he was in bad shape,
for exposure and loss of blood had robbed him of his
strength. It would take a while to build it back.

"We'll get a wagon, Bob," I told him, "maybe one of
those army ambulances. We can carry our grub in it,
and you too. This Wyoming air and a lot of buffalo
steaks will put you back in shape in no time."

Handy Corbin walked with me to the hotel and we
got us a room. Come daybreak, we'd be going back to
the herd, and would be driving north to the Hole-in-

the-Wall country. If we took short drives the first few days, Tarlton might be able to drive the wagon, leaving the four of us to handle the herd. It was not enough, but so far we hadn't found another hand. We could have used two or three more.

Folks in the hotel looked sharp at me when I came in, and more than one of them glanced at my empty holster, but nobody said anything. The crowd who'd been around the saloons had mostly gone home or to wherever they slept, and the folks I now saw were a different sort—men who'd been working, and up late . . . good people, for the most part.

The hotelkeeper, too, gave me a sharp look. "I'll deny no man a place to sleep, but I want no trouble, do you understand?"

"Mister," I said, "you're looking at a man who's had more than trouble enough. All I want is a few hours' sleep."

Then I went to the register and started to sign my name. The name in the space right above it was Martin Brimstead.

I did not even look at the other names. All I could see was that name, which seemed as if it was burned into the page.

Stud Pelly was a brute; but whatever Stud had done, he would not have done if Brimstead had lifted a hand to stop him. Stud might have held the rope, but it was Martin Brimstead who had hanged my pa.

And Martin Brimstead was here . . . in this hotel! Carefully, I replaced the pen.

Martin Brimstead had come west to speculate in Wyoming land . . . and now I was going to see that he got a piece of it. I was going to take particular care to see that he got the right piece, and of the right size.

It had to be about six feet long, and about three feet wide.

13

When I rolled out of bed the sun was already high in the sky. It was a bright, sunny morning. I pulled on my jeans and stomped my feet into my boots, and then headed for the washbasin. I could see that the first thing I needed was a razor and a shave.

When I went to the window I pulled back the curtain and looked up and down the street. Everything looked about as it should in a western town on a nice morning.

There were a dozen horses tied at the hitching rails, a buckboard stood in front of the bank, the team dozing in the warm sun. Farther down a wagon was being loaded. A few idlers loafed along the boardwalk, enjoying a morning smoke. Nothing seemed out of kilter.

Putting on my gunbelt with its empty holster, I checked my rifle and then put it carefully to one side. Only then did I realize that Corbin was gone.

The blankets and heavy comforter had been heaped in such a way that I'd paid his bed no mind, but now it bothered me that he had managed to get out of the room without me knowing. It showed how tired I'd been.

I lathered my face and shaved, and put everything carefully away. In the cold light of day I was having second thoughts about Martin Brimstead. A man like him would find trouble a-plenty in these western lands. If there was to be trouble with me, he must bring it on himself. Pa, I thought to myself, would not kill him.

Stud Pelly was a horse of another color. Stud was big and he was rough, but the years had done a few things for me. Besides giving me confidence, they had put some height on me, and some weight. I knew how to treat Stud Pelly, with the only medicine he'd understand.

This morning I slung my rifle from my left shoulder. I'd been experimenting and found I could get it into action a split second faster that way. The left hand would already be well up on the barrel when I swung the rifle forward, and the right hand would come naturally to the trigger.

When I walked into the restaurant, I stopped dead still. For right in front of me was Martin Brimstead, and seated at the table with him was Kitty Dunvegan . . . Kitty and Priss, her sister.

Brimstead looked up, and it took him a minute to recognize me. "Well," he said loudly, "the horse thief's boy!"

"No." I walked right up to his table. "The son of the man you helped to murder." I leaned on the table. "Let me tell you something, Brimstead. In this country what you just said to me is an invitation to a shooting. The next time you open your mouth about me, or about my pa, you better be wearing a gun."

He reddened with anger, and then as he realized what I'd said, rather than who was saying it, his face paled a little.

Glancing at Kit, I said, "Hello, Kit. Where's your pa?"

She was not the long-legged, freckled girl I had known—she was beautiful.

"Pa's dead, Otis Tom," she said. "He died last year."

"I was figuring on coming back yonder, come spring. I was hoping to see you."

Priss spoke suddenly. "Kit wouldn't want to see you, or anyone like you. I'll have you know she's going to marry Mr. Brimstead." I had never liked Priss, and liked her less now.

Kit's face was white, and she looked stiff and scared. I stared at her. "You don't mean that," I said. "Not him."

"Yes, she is going to marry me," Brimstead said. "And I'll thank you to leave my table. *At once!*"

I looked at him. "Brimstead, when I heard last night that you were in town, I went to bed with one idea. To get up this morning, hunt you down, and kill you. When I woke up this morning I told myself you were carrion. You weren't worth the trouble. I'd be wasting lead I might use to kill a coyote or a skunk. So don't you make me change my mind. You just set there quiet, and you can stay. Open your fat mouth again, and you'll get the back of my hand."

Coolly, I pulled back a chair and sat down. There were a dozen people in the restaurant, all seeming to ignore us, but I knew they'd heard every word.

"I was coming back for you, Kit. You knew I was coming back, didn't you?"

"I hoped you were."

Then, coolly and with sudden defiant glances at her sister, she explained. "Pa owed Mr. Brimstead money . . . quite a lot. At least, Mr. Brimstead had papers that said pa owed him, although I never saw any of the money and I don't believe that pa did.

"He wanted to marry me after his wife died, and Priss told me it was the only way we could pay him— else he'd take our place. I refused.

"Then there was all this talk about land in Wyoming. We'd had two very dry years, everything was burned up and dried up, and people were planning to move out west. Mr. Brimstead was coming out to buy land. He said we could come with him, and all I could think of was that it was a chance to get away from the valley, and I knew you were somewhere out here. So I came west."

"It isn't every day a girl gets a chance to marry a man like Martin Brimstead," Priss said to me, "and you've got no right to come barging in here making trouble."

"You like him, you marry him," I told her. "Kit is going to marry me."

"I'd like that, Otis Tom," Kit said. "I surely would. I've wanted nothing so much since first I saw you."

Folks around us were grinning. They were liking Kit, and they felt that I was western. Brimstead was from the East, and he had a manner they didn't take to. They were enjoying the show, and I didn't blame them in the least.

"Now, see here!" Brimstead began, but I just looked at him.

"You set down, Brimstead . . . or whatever your name is."

That one hit the mark. It got him in the wind, and for the first time I really believed that story I'd heard —that Brimstead wasn't his real name. He sagged back into his chair as if he'd been punched in the belly, and he sat there staring at his hands on the table before him.

"I'm in the cattle business," I said, "with one herd in the Hole-in-the-Wall country, another herd just outside town. I've got a good partner . . . he's been a cattle buyer for the eastern market. I'll be driving north when I've finished my business here."

Seeing Kit had made me forget where I was, and who was in town, but suddenly I remembered, and I glanced toward the door. There was no one there.

Somewhere in town I had enemies, and unless Handy Corbin was so inclined, I had not a friend to help me.

"Get your things, Kit," I said. "If you'll have me, we'll be married tomorrow."

"I'll have you, Otis Tom. Oh, I'll have you, all right,

and it would be a happy day for pa if he were here to see it."

"You talk like a fool!" Priss flared. "After all I've done for you, to leave a man like Martin Brimstead and take up with a no-account."

"Martin who?" I suggested quietly. "Now, look, ma'am. He spoke of me as a horse thief's son, so it's only fair to ask who *he* is. But you ask him, Priss. We don't care." I pushed back my chair and stood up. "Coming, Kit?"

She got up, standing fair and tall before me, trim as a clipper ship. Would I dare take her to the Hole-in-the-Wall? Then, looking into those proud, brave eyes, I knew she would never stay behind. Where I had the courage to go, there she would go also.

When she paused at the foot of the stairs that led to the rooms above, I warned her. "There are men out there a-looking for me, Kit. They are men I have to meet. Remember this: if anything should go wrong, Bob Tarlton, at the doctor's office now, is my partner. He knows about you, and you're to have all that's mine."

"Is it that bad, then?"

"It's that bad, Kit. They are dangerous men, killing men, but I am a fair hand with this." I touched my rifle. "And I've a lot to live for. I'll be meeting you, but I'd be a poor man to tie to if I didn't think of what might come. So stay off the street until I come for you."

"You're going to look for them?"

"For Queenie, the girl that's with them. She's a bad lot, Kit, but I'd like her to tell the marshal about that killing when I got the ivory-handled gun. She was there, and she saw it. She is the only one who can clear me . . . there are some in this town right now who believe me guilty."

It was warm in the street that day, warm and sunny, with the gray, silvery boards of the walk hot under foot. Men leaned against the awning posts, smoking limp cigarettes and squinting their eyes against the

Cheyenne sun—men who only the night before had been looking to hang me . . . at least, some of them.

They looked at me now, and their eyes were cold. Here and there a few might reserve opinion, but they all knew I was free only on condition, and that the matter was not resolved. I also knew, too, that with the coming of night when they got together to talk, and had a few drinks under their belts, they might be out to look for me again.

Pausing briefly before a store window, I glanced at the tall young man reflected there. Yes, I had come a good distance since that day in the village when they had hung pa. My shoulders were broad, and I was strong . . . stronger than most men. Yet the distance I had come was only a fraction of where I had to go to become the man I wished to be.

Suddenly hard boots sounded on the walk, and a loud, bullying voice said, "Hell! There's that horse thief's boy! Looks as if they're weaving a rope for you, boy, just like for your pa."

He stood there before me, and he was big, even bigger than I had expected—broad and thick and strong. There was a stubble of beard on his face, and his small, cruel eyes were sneering at me, his red lips holding the stub of a cigar. It was Stud Pelly.

There was only one language that Stud understood, but it was a language I knew how to speak.

Turning my head, I saw a cowhand lazing against the rail. He had a tough, wedge-like face, and cool, measuring eyes. He looked down-at-heel and dust-covered, but I liked the look of him.

"*Amigo,*" I said, "I have enemies around town. Would you keep them off my back while I tidy up a bit?"

I handed him my rifle, and unfastened my gunbelt, with its empty holster. He took them from me, not smiling, but his eyes went to Stud. "You're taking in a wide belt of country, friend," he said. "Luck to you."

Pelly stood there, his cigar in his teeth, chuckling.

"You don't really mean you're goin' to try to fight me?" he said, as if he couldn't believe it. "You're not somebody to fight, you're somebody to spank!"

"Spank me, then," I said, and hit him.

I mean I tried . . . but I missed. I'd forgotten how good he really was, for he'd served his time on the river boats, where it was knuckle-and-skull until who flung the chunk. I swung, but I was too confident, and when I missed he flattened me. I mean something exploded alongside my head—that hamlike fist of Stud's —and I hit the dust as if I'd been thrown from a sunfishing bronc.

No sooner did my back strike the ground than panic hit me. He was coming for me, and I knew what he could do with those boots of his. I rolled over, came up with a lunge, and he kicked me in the chest. I went down again, knocked well back, and he rushed at me, his body a solid chunk of beef and bone.

Again I came up and again I went down, and then he rushed me to put his boots to my head and guts. I lunged at him and he spilled over me. He was up as fast as I was and dove at me, head down and charging, meaning to butt me over. I'd heard about that skull of his; he boasted he could break down an oak door with it, and I turned just in time, so he missed me and I tripped him up.

I stood back as he got up, not from fair play but simply to catch my wind. He came at me again, feinting a charging butt, but suddenly looping a heavy overhand right at me. That was more my style and I let it go over my shoulder and smashed a short one to the wind. It was the first time I'd hit him, and I think he was surprised, but he clinched and tried to back-heel me.

He had me off balance and I was going down, so I simply kicked up the other foot and fell, thowing up my feet as I hit the ground. He went over me, and I gave a great shove with my hands and he fell free. I came up fast and caught him on the rise with a right that pulped his lips.

He put the back of his hand to his mouth and stared at the blood, then he came at me, slowly, hands poised to grapple. I feinted, but he did not take the offer, coming right on at me. I stepped back, and back. Suddenly I realized the boardwalk was behind me and that in a moment I'd be flat on my back, so I stepped in, punched to the side of his neck; and when he tried to rush me back so I'd trip, I hooked a short one to his ear.

We stood there then, looking at each other. "How do you like it, Stud?" I said. "Don't welch on me now. I'm going to put a reef in your lip." My right hand was moving but I jabbed with my left, a solid, bone-jarring blow to the mouth, that sore mouth that was already mashed. Blood started to flow, and he dove at me, swinging his short, powerful arms in hooking blows that hurt, every one of them. I braced my legs and let him come, and moved in at the last instant and grabbed by the belt, front and side, and twisting, whirled him around, smashing him head-on into the hitch rail.

The rail broke under the impact, and he sat there stunned, while I stood back, getting my breath.

There must have been a hundred people standing about by now, cheering us on. Pelly got up and staggered a little, but he wasn't hurt as much as I'd hoped, for he bulled into me suddenly, going under my punch and butting me in the belly. I felt a stabbing pain and my breath left me in a grunt. I hit the dirt, but was saved by his own weight, which carried him by me.

My breath was gone, but I struggled up, backing off to catch my wind. He came in, slower this time, planning to finish me off, and I let him come. He was bleeding now from a scalp cut too, where his skull had met the rail.

I backed off, gasping, and he closed in. He hit me with a heavy left, pushed me into position with another left, and drew back his massive right fist. Then I moved. I knocked his left aside with my right forearm and chopped down with the right fist, catching him on the cheekbone. Then I threw myself into him, butting him in the face, and grabbing his belt, threw him as I had before. This time he went into the dust.

He was up with a lunge and I hit him left and right in the face, and he went down again. He was slower getting up now, and when he was up I feinted to bring his hands up, and I uppercut to his wind. He bent far over and I chopped down with a hammer blow at his kidney. He screamed, and straightened up, his mouth wide with agony, and I took a full swing at his jaw with a roundhouse left and smashed it. I could hear the bone break, and saw the lower part of his face go askew.

The blow turned him half around and I walked in, put a hand on his shoulder and uppercut to his belly. He started to fall, but I held him up and hit him again.

He went down into the dust, and I turned him over with my boot. "Stud," I said, "the next time you want to take a rope out and hang a man, you remember this little mix-up. When you're able, you leave town. You go back to Tennessee and tell them what happened, and if I ever see you again, I'll whip you again."

Then I walked back to the cowhand who held my rifle and gunbelt. He handed them to me.

"Figured he had you pullin' leather there at first," he said, "but you stayed with him."

"Thanks," I said, and then I looked at him again. "You working, or rustling work?"

"You hiring?"

"I want a man who can ride, handle cattle, and fight if need be."

"Well," he said, "I can fight and ride and handle cattle if need be. That suit you?"

"You just went to work," I said.

14

He walked into the hotel with me, and I washed up in a room back of the bar. I had a welt on my cheekbone and my knuckles were sore from the beating I'd given Pelly. By daybreak I'd be feeling all the sore spots.

"You're Otis Tom Chancy," my new cowhand said. "I'm Juniper Cogan. They call me June for short."

He watched me pull down my sleeves, button them, and then get into my vest again. "Otis Tom Chancy, you're one hell of a fist-fighter, but when you go out on the street again you'd better be good with a gun."

"What do you know?"

"Only what the town's talking. Caxton Kelsey is in town, LaSalle Prince and Andy Miller with him. They're gunning for you."

"There were two other men and a woman. What became of them?"

"The woman's right in this hotel . . . got a room on the street. The other two men were Phillips and Gassner, two-by-four rustlers." He rolled a smoke. "You got any other friends?"

So I told him about Tarlton, Handy Corbin, and the men riding with the cattle. "Better let me go get them," he said. "You can always round up the herd if they scatter."

"Uh-uh. We need those cattle, and we're starting north right away. You go on out and hold them. I'll come out when this is over."

He looked at me, incredulous. "You going to tackle them alone?"

"It's my fight, isn't it?"

Thoughtfully, I worked my fingers. My fists had taken quite a beating in the fight. Would my hands stiffen too much? Still, I wasn't going to rely on a six-shooter, but on the rifle.

"Look," I said, "there's one thing you can do." I dug two gold eagles from my pocket. "Take these down to the hardware store and buy me a six-gun. The best one they have."

When he had gone I went up to my room. Right now I needed rest. I propped a chair under the doorknob, pulled off my boots and gunbelt, and stretched out on the bed with my rifle near my hand. I needed to relax, but I also needed to do some contemplating.

Caxton Kelsey was no fool. He had no doubts as to his ability to take me in a gun battle, but the way I saw it he wasn't likely to take any chances at all. There were people in town who still believed I had done the Burgess murder; and I was free simply because all the evidence they had was my possession of Burgess' gun, and because folks in Cheyenne knew Bob Tarlton—some of them knew him in person, some by reputation—and with a good many western men that association cleared me of any guilt. Tarlton had a reputation as a good man and a good citizen, but just the same if Kelsey killed me a lot of people would say it was good riddance.

Kelsey would try to set this one up, I was sure. He would try to have me boxed so I'd have no chance. The thing I would have to do would be to get the jump on him. Instead of facing them all at once, on their own ground, I'd have to take them one or two at a time.

Since Queenie was in this hotel, it was likely Kelsey and the others were here too, or close by. The first thing I must do was learn where they were.

But with all this contemplating, I was tired enough that in a few moments I fell asleep.

A gentle tapping roused me. Glancing at my big silver watch, I saw I'd been asleep more than an hour. I swung my feet to the floor and stepped over beside the door, rifle in hand.

"*Si?*" I said, using Spanish, which an enemy would not expect.

"It's me, boss. June Cogan."

Moving the chair back with my left hand, I tipped my Winchester to cover the crack in the door and said, "All right, open it and come in slow."

It was Cogan, all right. And Handy Corbin was with him.

"Looks like you roped yourself a maverick," I said to Cogan. "Where'd you dab a loop on this one?"

"He rounded me up," Cogan said, grinning. "Seems like word gets around, and he heard you'd hired me."

"You've got your problems," Corbin said; "I've got mine. And my problem is LaSalle Prince. I've been trying for days to cut him loose from the herd so we can settle a matter."

"I heard he was kin of yours."

"Well, there's a matter of blood-line. It ends right there. The only kin he's got, run with the wolf packs who have the same kind of nature. He killed my brother . . . shot him for money."

"Where are they now?" I asked.

He told me that only Queenie was in the hotel. Phillips and Gassner were down on the street. Andy Miller was at the livery stable. LaSalle Prince was in the saloon across the way.

"Where's Kelsey?"

"You've got me. I figured you might know. Looks to

me as if they're waitin' for you to come out, Chancy. This time they don't figure on your gettin' out of town."

"Corbin, I'm driving my herd up to the Hole. I'm getting married tomorrow and my wife is going with me, and I don't intend for any no-account gunmen to keep me from it. Nor do I intend to sit here waitin' for them. You say Andy's at the stable? All right, I'll go down and have a talk with him."

"You're crazy! He's all set up for you."

"More than likely he's waiting for me to show up on the street so he can bottle me up, with Prince and those two out there to help, and Kelsey to come in on the kill. He won't be expecting me, but if he is I'm going to give him his chance."

"What do you want us to do?"

"Keep them off my back. That's all. This is my party."

"Not Prince. I've been hunting LaSalle Prince for two years."

"You can have him. Just don't let him get in my way."

The new six-shooter Cogan had bought for me was a beautiful piece of workmanship. After checking the gun, I loaded it from a fresh box of shells, and dropped it into my holster, which was now on my right thigh. Taking up my rifle, I went to the door. "You boys can keep an eye on Gassner and Phillips," I said. "I am going after Miller."

There was no longer any choice. To take a wife into Indian country was bad enough, but with the threat of an attack by outlaws too it was too much. I was going to give Andy Miller the chance of leaving me alone or shooting it out.

He was a fast, accurate man with a gun. Although most men would agree that he was not in Kelsey's class, he was a dangerous man. I had no desire to be known as a good man with a gun. All I wanted now was freedom to live, to raise my cattle, and to build the kind of home I'd always wanted.

Brimstead was out of the picture. He was a cruel, tyrannical man, but such men dig their own graves, and I felt no urge to be the man to top it off. I had whipped Stud Pelly, and Brimstead was no longer a danger to me.

The Kelsey outfit had tried to kill me. They had knocked me on the head and left me for dead, they had stolen our cattle, and they had come here to hunt me down.

I walked along the hall, and went down the back stairs to the area behind the buildings.

There was a scattering of lean-to sheds and out-houses, a couple of corrals, and open grass country dotted with a few shacks. Holding the Winchester in my right hand, I walked along, stepping over bottles, broken shingles, piles of firewood, and the usual truck that is left behind buildings in a hastily constructed town that has not taken the time to clean up.

Inside, I was empty, still. I was walking toward a shoot-out with a very dangerous man, and I told myself I was a fool. I should avoid this, could have avoided it. But it would eventually catch up with me . . . and I was not good at waiting for an axe to fall.

The livery stable was a huge, cavernous building, already weather-beaten. Behind it sprawled corrals and outbuildings. It fronted on the main street; inside there was an open space that separated the two lines of stalls. Above the stalls was the hayloft, now almost filled with hay.

Near the corrals in the rear were several freight wagons scattered over a vacant lot. While I was in the shadow beside one of the wagons it came over me what I was really tackling. Andy Miller was a skilled hand with a gun, who had used one many more times than I had. Not that I was any tenderfoot, for I'd grown up using shooting irons of one kind or another, but this was a mighty fast, tricky man I was going up against. And if somehow I came out of this one alive, there was still Kelsey.

Pausing beside the wagon, I took off my hat and wiped the hatband; after replacing it, I removed the thong from my six-shooter. Was I stalling? For a moment longer I hesitated. The sun was already going down, and it would soon be dusk. I could hear footsteps along the walks as people started for home, or for the restaurants for their evening meal. Farther away I heard a bugle sounding the mess call.

Stepping through the bars of the corral, I went across to the barn. I could smell dust, hay, and the usual barnyard odors. Having opened the gate and closed it carefully behind me, I walked across the dozen yards that separated me from the wide-open door of the stable.

The area between the rows of stalls was empty except for a man who sat at the street door, smoking a pipe. It was almost dark back in the stalls, but I could see the whites of the horses' eyes as they rolled them around at me. With the Winchester slung from my left shoulder, I went forward, eyes swinging right and left. Expecting a burst of gunfire at every step, I reached the street door, and the hostler looked up.

"Howdy! You're a soft-moving man. I never even heard you coming."

"I'm looking for Andy Miller."

He shot me a quick glance. "I'd give that some thought, boy. Not many folks go huntin' grief, thataway. Andy waited around a while, then went yonder up the street. Was I you, I'd mount up and ride whilst you're able."

Without replying to him, I started up the street, my left hand on the barrel of the Winchester. There was nothing in the way but a chicken, pecking at something that lay in the dust. When I came to the near end of the boardwalk I stepped up on it and walked along, keeping my eyes a-studying the buildings on either side, but also watching out for what lay ahead.

Just about then I noticed that not everybody had gone to supper. Phillips and Gassner were still standing on the street, and when they heard my boots on the boards they looked my way, and both of them crossed the street to the front of the hotel and waited there, watching me without seeming to. There was no sign of Corbin or Cogan.

The saloon where LaSalle Prince was said to have been was only a few doors farther along. So it should be some place right soon, if this was a trap they'd laid.

Suddenly I saw a narrow gap between the next two buildings and did a quick side step into it and stopped.

It was a moment before they realized I'd gone. Then I heard a startled exclamation, followed by the quick sound of boots. They came running, with Phillips a step in advance, Gassner on his left. I was waiting for them, and as they came into the opening I jabbed the muzzle of my rifle into the pit of Phillips' stomach, and then dropped Gassner with a butt stroke on the skull.

He fell as if struck by lightning, for it had been a solid blow. Phillips had staggered against the wall, holding his stomach with both hands and gasping helplessly for air, so I tunked him, too, on the skull with the rifle butt. Then I drew their guns, emptied them, and tossed them far back into the refuse and debris behind the buildings.

Not ten seconds had elapsed since they had reached the opening, and now I waited for what would come next.

The minutes ticked by slowly. Neither one of the men moved, but I was not concerned with them. Desperately, I was hoping my enemies would come into the open. My eyes went to the back of the passage, then back again to the street opening.

When nothing happened, I stepped out of the opening with my Winchester slung back to my shoulder, muzzle down, my hand hanging beside it. The street was empty.

Stepping away from the opening, I strolled up the walk . . . and suddenly they were there.

Caxton Kelsey came out of the hotel door and walked three steps toward me. I could hear the faint jingle of his spurs, the creak of the boards. The sun was down now, but it was still light enough to see. He stood on the edge of the boardwalk, smiling at me. He was a handsome man, standing there like that. It was no wonder Queenie was taken by him.

At that moment there was a rustle of movement above me, and I automatically glanced up. Andy Miller was on the balcony right above Kelsey, but a little to the left. And if LaSalle Prince was still in that saloon, he would be almost behind me. So they had me boxed, after all.

There was a great stillness in the street. The slightest sound could be heard. I was conscious of the coolness of the breeze, drying the sweat on my forehead; I was conscious of the deepening shadow under the awning behind Kelsey. Somewhere a dog yelped . . . a horse at the hitch rail stamped a foot.

Caxton Kelsey stood there calm and confident. "Well, Chancy," he said, "we've had to wait a while, but we've got you."

Kelsey was the one I had to get. I couldn't shoot at both at once, and Kelsey was the more dangerous one. Also, I knew that shooting downward, as Andy Miller would have to do, was a chancy thing. Many a shot has been missed by a man shooting downhill. Kelsey was the one I had to take, and then Miller, if luck was with me.

"Now, Mr. Kelsey," I said, "you boys sure enough came a long way hunting for something most folks try to avoid. And I figure you're seeing things from kind of a one-sided viewpoint. You say you've got me boxed, but are you right sure the shoe isn't on the other foot?

"Take Andy up there—I never did see a man more anxious to be a target. He's standing right up there in front of everybody."

I was playing for time. I wanted the jump on them the way they had tried to get it on me. That I had friends in town was true, but I had no idea any of them were within blocks of me right now. But these two surely didn't know that, and I had to put a burr under their saddle just to worry them a mite.

"And don't you expect help from LaSalle Prince, because he's going to have problems of his own in just about a minute. So it looks like you and me, Kelsey— and how about *now!*"

His hand slapped his gun butt, but my Winchester barrel lifted in my left hand, my right hand fired the rifle from belt-high, and my bullet caught Kelsey on the belt buckle, glancing up to strike his chest.

The blow knocked him back, and I tilted my rifle just as Andy Miller fired, taking a step forward and triggering as my foot hit ground. His shot missed, and my rifle shot truer at that range. He toppled forward, hit the edge of the roof, and rolled over, falling to the street.

Behind me in the saloon I heard a hammering of gunshots, but I could not think of those, for Kelsey was getting up, bloody and savage. He swung his gun on me and we both fired. Something hit me a wallop that staggered me, but I worked the lever on the Winchester again, and fired again. He was leaning against the water trough, with one leg spraddled out, and there was blood on his chest and his face.

The shooting behind me ceased. Rifle held waist-high, I circled into the street. Caxton Kelsey was still a fighting man, and he was grinning at me. "Why, I didn't think you had it in you, Chancy," he said. "Too bad you have to die." He was bringing his pistol up.

I could see the silver belt buckle bent out of shape, and the blood on his chest, but it didn't look as if he was badly hurt. My bullet, in glancing upward, might have just cut the skin on his chest. Where the other two bullets had hit—and I was sure they had—I did not know. He seemed to be half supporting himself against the water trough.

We were not over sixty feet apart, and I was cross-

ing the street in a sort of half-circle, swinging away
from him. At that distance my rifle was considerably
more accurate, but he was a noted shot, and at sixty
feet could do terrible destruction with the gun he held.

He watched me, gun balanced in his hand, waiting
to make the killing shot. To pause, to sight along the
barrel at him, would give him just the moment he
needed, so I kept moving.

There was no sound on the street. The evening light
seemed to hold, and the sun touched only the roof tops.
I was conscious of the silence, of the dust, of the sense
of waiting. We were alone . . . as alone as if we stood
in the desert . . . each of us playing for time, each
wanting the next shot to be the last.

There had been shooting in the saloon—had Handy
Corbin killed Prince? Or was Prince even now nearing
a door to take a shot at my back? Above all, where
was Queenie? In the restaurant I heard a subdued rattle
of dishes.

Kelsey had gradually eased himself around the corner
of the water trough on which he had leaned. One knee
had lowered to the ground, and on his left side the
hitching rail and the post were a partial shield.

"I have no pity for you, Kelsey," I said. "No more
than you had for Noah Gates and his men."

"What were they?" he asked contemptuously. "Just
old men, worn out with years and trouble."

"But," I said, "they were men who did what they
could to make a living, and not to steal it from other
men. What have you done, Kelsey? Have you done an
honest day's work in ten years?"

"Work is for the sheep," he said. "I run with the
wolves."

His gun barrel seemed to be lifting, ever so little,
but if I were farther to the left he would have to shift
his gun around the post to be in line for a shot.

Suddenly I ran. Three quick steps to the right . . . I
stopped, and he shot. He had shifted the gun to line on
me, but he fired too quickly. The shot bellowed against

the wooden wall of the building, and missed. I felt the whip of it as I fired my rifle.

My bullet spat slivers from the post. I worked the lever, dropped quickly to one knee, and fired again. I saw the dust leap from his jacket, and his bullet threw dust in front of me. I started to lunge to my feet, but went suddenly weak and sprawled in the dust, still frantically working the lever.

Caxton Kelsey was up. Bloody and staggering, he was on his feet, lining his pistol at me as I lay there. Rolling over, I came to one knee and fired into him. His bullet hit the top of my shoulder, and I felt the sharp, angry burn of it. Then I fired again.

He stood an instant, the gun dangling from his fingers, then he sat down abruptly, staring at nothing. And then he simply lay down and rolled over.

Crouching there, I held my rifle ready, watching him. In a moment, using the rifle for a crutch, I pushed myself to my feet and took a step to the edge of the walk, where I sat down hard, gripping the rifle, still watching Kelsey.

People began to appear on the street, and Handy Corbin was suddenly pushing through them. He crossed the street to me.

"You got him! By the Lord Harry, you got him! They were offerin' ten-to-one odds and no takers that he'd gun you down!"

"What about Prince?" I asked.

Handy Corbin shrugged, and looked away uncomfortably. "You got to understand that, boss," he said, almost apologetically. "He was one of our own, and it was up to me to do. We're good folks, mostly, and we aim to do right. LaSalle was no good—right from the start there was something cross-grained about him. He was forever a-tryin' to lead us boys into trouble. Two, three times as he was growin' up pa got him out of trouble, but it seemed like he got wilder and meaner.

"Then a neighbor of ours sold some sheep, and La-

Salle met him on the road and LaSalle had a bottle. The
two of them got to drinkin', and first thing you know
that neighbor woke up with a thick head and his money
gone. LaSalle, he began spendin' down at the corners,
and we knew what must have happened. That man
braced him with it, and LaSalle shot him. Didn't kill
him, but hurt him bad, and then LaSalle, he taken out.

"Next thing we knew he was off buffalo huntin', but
he spent more time huntin' buffalo hunters than buffalo.
He sold a team of grays in Cherry Creek, Colorado,
that had belonged to a couple of brothers working out
of Abilene. Somebody recognized the horses, and later
the bodies were found. LaSalle, he became an outlaw.
He went from that to killin' for hire, and we figured
we'd turned loose a mad wolf on the country, and it
was up to us to slow him down. Pa, he saddled up and
rode off to have a talk with him.

"LaSalle, he laughed at pa. Said he was a sancti-
monious old fool, and told him to go on back home
whilst he was able. Pa wasn't about to take that off no
man, and he told LaSalle to take off his guns, because
he was sure enough goin' to whup him. Pa stripped off
his guns, and then LaSalle drew one of his and shot pa.
He shot him in the knee, and he fell, and when he tried
to get up, he shot him in the other. He cussed pa out,
then killed him. So I've been huntin' him ever since,
and teachin' myself to be fast enough to beat him."

Me, I was beginning to get the reaction now, the let-
down that comes after. I didn't want to talk, I wanted
to get in somewhere off the street. Corbin helped me
down to the Doc's office, where Bob Tarlton was
a-pacing the floor. He'd heard the shooting—in fact, it
woke him from a nap he was taking. The Doc was there
and wouldn't let him go out on the street.

It felt good just to stretch out on that table, for I
was all in. That was one time I'd not have given a
plugged nickel for Otis Tom Chancy's possibilities, and
nobody knew better than me how lucky I'd been.

As it was, I'd caught a slug through the shoulder that

missed the bone. I had a deep furrow across the top of the shoulder, and at least two bullet burns I didn't even recall getting. I'd lost some blood and a whole lot of steam.

But the thing that worried me now was Kit. There was no sign of her, but she might be hunting me right then.

"Handy," I said, "you go down to the hotel and find Miss Dunvegan. Tell her I'm all right."

The Doc looked around. "She was around here earlier, Chancy. She had that cowhand of yours, Juniper Cogan. She was hunting the marshal."

The marshal? Where had he been, anyway? Was he like some of those cowtown marshals who preferred to see trouble shoot itself out? Some of them never lifted a hand, as long as the town's citizens were left alone.

Well, I started to get up and the Doc pushed me down. "You lie still. You may not be shot up as bad as I expected, but you've lost a lot of blood and you're weaker than a cat."

Tarlton got up. "I'll go with him, Otis. You rest easy now. . . . Who did you say the girl was?"

"Her name is Kitty Dunvegan, and she's pretty as all get out. Come noontime tomorrow, we're getting married."

"We'll find her then," Tarlton said. "But I know June Cogan, and if she's with him she'll be all right."

15

They left me alone there, with the lamp wick turned low, lying up in bed with a lot of weakness and some pain, and a mighty wish to be up and doing that faded as tiredness set in.

It seemed as if I'd been going at top pace as long as I could recall, and there was nothing for it but to rest now.

It worried me that Kit Dunvegan was in that wild western town, maybe alone and without protection. I should have known they bred them strong in Tennessee, for Kit was a girl with a mind of her own, and ideas of her own.

Finally I put a hand above the lamp chimney and blew out the light. I could smell the smoldering wick for a few minutes, and then I must have slept, for when I opened my eyes again, Kit was sitting there in a chair beside the bed reading a book, and it was clear daylight beyond the curtains.

For several minutes I said nothing, just enjoying the look of her there, sitting so prim and still, turning the leaves of her book. Looking back, I could scarcely recall when last a woman had sat at my bedside, and then it was ma, when I was a sick boy. . . .

She turned her head and met my eyes, and for a moment we looked at each other, not speaking, and then she jumped up. "The doctor said you were to have some hot broth when you woke up."

"Where were you? I was worried."

She ran her hands down her apron, smoothing it. "I went to see Queenie Gates."

"You *what?*"

"I really didn't think she was all that pretty . . . hard-looking, sort of."

"You went to see that she-cat? Don't you realize you could have been hurt?"

"By her?" She looked disdainful. "I could handle her. But I took the marshal along, and Juniper Cogan. I wanted some witnesses."

"To what?"

"To a deposition. If we were going to bring charges against you for shooting that man back in the Nation, we had to have evidence, didn't we? Naturally, if he was my uncle I'd want you punished, wouldn't I?"

"You told her that?"

"Well . . . I implied it. It wasn't actually said. But we had to have her sworn account of the gun battle, and she was very anxious to give us all the information she had. How he was armed and all, but you shot him without giving him a chance."

"That's not true."

"Of course, we had her describe the weapon . . . we wanted that for evidence, you know, because you were in possession of the gun. She described the ivory-handled gun in detail. Swore to her evidence, and June and the marshal witnessed it."

What could I say to that? While I was busy stalking Andy Miller, she was making her own plans and carrying them out.

"Where were you when the shooting started?" I asked.

"In her room . . . at the door, in fact. We were just leaving."

Kit went to the other room and returned with the broth. Then she went on with her story.

"Queenie said, 'You needn't have bothered. Chancy won't live to see prison. Kelsey will kill him.'

"I couldn't resist telling her then, so I said, 'Otis Tom won't die that easy, Mrs. Gates. You'll see. I've known him since I was a little girl.'

"Well, you should have seen her face. She caught up the empty water pitcher and threw it at me, but Mr. Cogan jerked the door shut . . . just in time. I'm afraid she was very angry."

Bob Tarlton came in about then. He was up and about, although looking mighty thin. "Juniper Cogan and Handy went out to the herd," he said. "We're starting them north in the morning, if that's all right with you."

"Sure. I'll be up—"

"Not you . . . us. The doctor says I can ride part of the day for a while, if I rest in the wagon. You won't be up to it for several days yet, and we sort of figured you and Kit might want to honeymoon down to Denver or somewhere."

Now, who could argue against a setup like that? Not me, at least.

Kit, she wasn't doing any arguing either.

ABOUT LOUIS L'AMOUR

"I think of myself in the oral tradition—as a troubadour, a village taleteller, the man in the shadows of the campfire. That's the way I'd like to be remembered—as a storyteller. A good storyteller."

It is doubtful that any author could be as at home in the world re-created in his novels as Louis Dearborn L'Amour. Not only could he physically fill the boots of the rugged characters he writes about, but he has literally "walked the land my characters walk." His personal experiences as well as his lifelong devotion to historical research have combined to give Mr. L'Amour the unique knowledge and understanding of the people, the events, and the challenge of the American frontier that have become the hallmarks of his popularity.

Of French-Irish descent, Mr. L'Amour can trace his own family in North America back to the early 1600s and follow their steady progression westward, "always on the frontier." As a boy growing up in Jamestown, North Dakota, he absorbed all he could about his family's frontier heritage, including the story of his great-grandfather who was scalped by Sioux warriors.

Spurred by an eager curiosity and desire to broaden his horizons, Mr. L'Amour left home at the age of fifteen and enjoyed a wide variety of jobs including seaman, lumberjack, elephant handler, skinner of dead cattle, assessment miner, and officer on tank destroyers during World War II. During his "yondering" days he also circled the world on a freighter, sailed a dhow on the Red Sea, was shipwrecked in the West Indies and stranded in the Mojave Desert. He has won fifty-one of fifty-nine fights as a professional boxer and worked as a journalist and lecturer. A voracious reader and collector of rare books, Mr. L'Amour's personal library of some 10,000 volumes covers a broad range of scholarly disciplines including many personal papers, maps, and diaries of the pioneers.

Mr. L'Amour "wanted to write almost from the time I could walk." After developing a widespread following for his many adventure stories written for the fiction magazines, Mr. L'Amour published his first full-length novel, *Hondo*, in 1953. Mr. L'Amour is now one of the four bestselling living novelists in the world. Every one of his more than 95 books are still in print and every one has sold more than one million copies. He has more million-copy bestsellers than any other living author. His books have been translated into more than a dozen languages, and more than thirty of his novels and stories have been made into feature films and television movies.

His hardcover bestsellers include *The Lonesome Gods; The Walking Drum*, his twelfth-century historical novel; *Jubal Sackett; Last of the Breed;* and *The Haunted Mesa.*

The recipient of many great honors and awards, in 1983 Mr. L'Amour became the first novelist ever to be awarded a Special National Gold Medal by the United States Congress in honor of his life's work. In 1984 he was also awarded the Medal of Freedom by President Ronald Reagan.

Mr. L'Amour lives in Los Angeles with his wife, Kathy, and their two children, Beau and Angelique.

Special Offer
Buy a Bantam Book
for only 50¢.

Now you can have Bantam's catalog filled with hundreds of titles plus take advantage of our unique and exciting bonus book offer. A special offer which gives you the opportunity to purchase a Bantam book for only 50¢. Here's how!

By ordering any five books at the regular price per order, you can also choose any other single book listed (up to a $5.95 value) for just 50¢. Some restrictions do apply, but for further details why not send for Bantam's catalog of titles today!

Just send us your name and address and we will send you a catalog!

BANTAM BOOKS, INC.
P.O. Box 1006, South Holland, Ill. 60473

Mr./Mrs./Ms. _____
(please print)

Address _____

City _____ State _____ Zip _____
FC(A)—10/87
Please allow four to six weeks for delivery.